The Minister's Restoration

The Minister's Restoration

George MacDonald

Michael R. Phillips, Editor

BETHANY HOUSE PUBLISHERS
MINNEAPOLIS, MINNESOTA 55438
A Division of Bethany Fellowship, Inc.

Cover illustration by Dan Thornberg,
Bethany House Publishers staff artist.

Originally published in 1897 as SALTED WITH FIRE
by Hurst & Blackett Publishers, London.

Published by Bethany House Publishers
A Division of Bethany Fellowship, Inc.
6820 Auto Club Road, Minneapolis, Minnesota 55438

Printed in the United States of America

Library of Congress Cataloging-in-Publication Data

MacDonald, George, 1824-1905.
   The minister's restoration.

   Rev. ed. of: Salted with fire. 1897.
   I. Phillips, Michael R., 1946-   .
II. MacDonald, George, 1824-1905. Salted with fire.
III. Title.
PR4967.S25   1988   823'.8   87-33813
ISBN 0-87123-905-1 (pbk.)

Scottish Romances by George MacDonald retold for today's reader by Michael Phillips

The two-volume story of Malcolm:
The Fisherman's Lady
The Marquis' Secret

Companion stories of Gibbie and his friend Donal:
The Baronet's Song
The Shepherd's Castle

Companion stories of Hugh Sutherland and Robert Falconer:
The Tutor's First Love
The Musician's Quest

Companion stories of Thomas Wingfold:
The Curate's Awakening
The Lady's Confession
The Baron's Apprenticeship

Stories that stand alone:
The Gentlewoman's Choice
The Highlander's Last Song
The Laird's Inheritance
The Maiden's Bequest
The Minister's Restoration

The George MacDonald Collector's Library—
beautifully bound hard-cover editions:
The Fisherman's Lady
The Marquis' Secret

A New Biography of George MacDonald by Michael Phillips

George MacDonald: Scotland's Beloved Storyteller

Contents

Introduction

The year was 1896. George MacDonald—Scottish novelist, poet, preacher, essayist, and lecturer—was reaching the end of a long and highly successful literary career. At 71 years of age, he had authored 51 books of a singularly diverse nature that had sold in the many millions of copies. He was held in the highest esteem as a scholar, a man of letters, and a gifted writer, as well as a spiritual sage. Some would have ventured to call him a prophet. Others spoke of his imaginative powers as genius.

Only a year previously his eerie *Lilith* had been released—that book which would come to be viewed by the critics as the crowning achievement to cap his distinguished life, that chilling fictional fantasy of death which various commentators have in retrospect viewed as a prelude to his own.

But now, a year later, the force of his imagination and concentration was gradually diminishing. He was able to travel but little. His days of teaching, lecturing, and writing were largely past. Many of the ailments which had stalked him throughout life were at last taking their toll. Three years later he would suffer the stroke that would effectively signal an end to his active life.

What then was left for this man, who had already done so much, to give to the world—a world that would in a very short time be able to remember him only through his books?

The answer to that question lies in the pages you are about to read. In that period between *Lilith* and the stroke which came at age 74, during the year 1896, George MacDonald sat down to write one last novel, which he called *Salted With Fire*.

A simple story, neither so long nor complex of plot and description as most of his earlier and lengthier novels, *Salted With Fire* somehow provides a fitting climax to MacDonald's historic and controversial career. Its essential themes echo in concise and straightforward manner those elements of fundamental spirituality that

9

MacDonald had been conveying through his books, his characters, his poems, his sermons, and his very life for over forty years.

Many aspects of the faith MacDonald so cherished found their way onto these pages, and from a whole variety of perspectives, *Salted With Fire* typifies the fiction of George MacDonald. Here again we encounter a minister (like Wingfold, Drake, Bevis, Cowie) wrestling with the truth and claims of the gospel as he must evaluate the foundations of his own relationship with God. As he does so, other familiar themes come to bear upon his troubled but searching heart—what is the nature of repentance, how exhaustive is God's forgiveness, what is the path to restoration with God and man, and what is the nature of the Love which will spare no pain to break through into an individual heart?

Here too we encounter the dialect of the best of MacDonald's Scottish novels. With delight we meet another memorable aging humble saint (reminding us particularly of Donal Grant's cobbler friend Andrew, as well as David Elginbrod, Alexander Graham, and Joseph Polwarth) who acts as spiritual mentor to those in need. There is the hearkening back to MacDonald's personal roots in Scotland; only six or seven miles southwest of MacDonald's hometown of Huntly is a tiny village called Tillathrowie which is quite possibly the setting for this story. The people and themes are agrarian, and we are strongly reminded of the intrinsic link in MacDonald's personal faith between his love for his homeland and his love for the Lord. And the final chapters of *Salted With Fire* provide a grand and victorious statement of the essence of faith, as MacDonald, now at the end of his life, viewed it—practical, living, growing, honest, and humble—rooted in the love of God that man must learn to choose as the best, indeed the only pathway into life.

The title of the book, perhaps as much as the contents themselves, gives us a window into George MacDonald's mind at the time he penned his tale. From the earliest stages of his career, George MacDonald found himself in theological difficulty with the fundamental Calvinist wing of Christendom because of his view of God's character. To the Calvinists, a sinner was lost, both in this life and in the life to come. To MacDonald, however, God's love was infinite, and extended itself toward all of creation, even potentially onto the other side of death if necessary, using whatever extremes of discipline and purposeful suffering as will open the eyes of repentance and cause His love to break through.

The very phrase "salted with fire" in so many ways capsulizes and provides a final and powerful statement of MacDonald's view of God's purifying and inescapable repentance-producing fire, which comes to bear in this story on young Blatherwick. Salt has long been both a practical and a spiritual symbol for and expression of purification. Thus, the very title of this book captures the theme of the whole, as does the quote from chapter fourteen: "There was no way around the purifying fire! He could not escape it; he *must* pass through it!"

Purification (salt) of the spirit comes through pain, through godly discipline, through searing repentance, through spiritual fire. Jesus said, "Everyone will be salted with fire," echoing the prophets Zechariah and Malachi, who said: "I will bring them into the fire: I will refine them like silver and test them like gold. They will call on my name and I will answer them" (Zech. 13:9) and, "But who can endure the day of his coming? . . . For he will be like a refiner's fire. . . . He will sit as a refiner and purifer of silver; he will purify the Levites and refine them like gold and silver" (Mal. 3:2–3).

It was scriptures such as these that George MacDonald felt revealed the true extent of God's love, harsh as they seemed on the surface, and the far-reaching purposefulness of His nature in all of life and even beyond death. Those who have attempted to categorize MacDonald through the years as a "liberal" (which he was to some), or a "conservative" (which he was to others) or a "universalist" (which he appeared to those who did not study his writings in sufficient depth), or a "heretic" (which he seemed to the staunch Calvinists of his day) have all largely missed the point in their attempts to pigeonhole him according to their pre-set standards. They overlook the intense hunger of his heart after God. They overlook the obedience and fruit of his life. For MacDonald, to this day, steadfastly resists all attempts to categorize him. His views do not fall neatly into any doctrinal "camp." He forged new theological ground by proposing entirely new and bold interpretations of many aspects of God's character, including: the purpose of the afterlife, of God's redemptive plan, of the deeper meaning of God's justice, of the limitlessness of the atonement, of the divine intent behind the purifying fire spoken of by the Old Testament prophets, and of the extent of God's ultimate victory over sin.

The title of this present book, therefore, as well as that of one of his well-known published sermons dealing with similar themes ("Our God Is a Consuming Fire"), in a sense pinpoints one of the key topics MacDonald felt keenly driven to communicate and which remained focal for him all his life. From his earliest days as a child, when he questioned God's condemnation of sinners, young George Mac-Donald grappled to come to grips with God's character and what His love entailed. As a youth he searched to integrate these questions into a consistent picture of God's love in harmony with His anger and justice. Finally as an adult he presented to the world a fully matured vision of a God of infinite love who was prepared to go to any lengths (even through the use of the purifying fire of His love) to redeem a man, to bring about repentance in the utter depths of his heart, and ultimately to heal and restore him and bring him back into fellowship with Him. It was convictions such as these that gave MacDonald such a victorious and visionary outlook concerning God's purposes, a vision communicated through his novels.

On an altogether different level, *Salted With Fire* speaks to the twentieth-century church about a problem as contemporary as today's newspapers and national events—sin, not only within the individual heart, but within the public ministry. Indeed, it is uncanny how prophetic MacDonald's subject matter is, written almost one hundred years ago, with respect to events that rocked evangelicalism in America last year. And through the characters of George MacDonald's creation can be found properly scriptural solutions. Here we find no leveling of charges by fellow Christians and fellow ministers, no breakdown of unity within the body over issues that make the ministry a mockery in the eyes of a watching world, no attempts to hide and deceive and twist the truth, no plays for power, no motives rooted in money, no national scandal, no conditional repentance.

One hundred years ago, George MacDonald offered a simple solution to sin according to the biblical standard that today's church would do so well to heed. A definite order exists toward a total and godly resolution. *Repentance* for the wrong done must precede all else. Following repentance comes *forgiveness*, of a threefold nature—forgiveness by God, forgiveness on the part of others, and forgiveness of self. Once these two vital foundation stones have been laid, there can come *healing*, which is based in stepping down and humbly laying aside all claim to position, wealth, influence, and reputation. Then at last can come, in God's time and God's way, *restoration*. How greatly could today's church learn how to apply these basic truths as taught in the last century by the author of *Salted With Fire*.

Working on *Salted With Fire* presented both unique challenges as well as unique rewards. I found this book more difficult in certain ways than perhaps any of the other MacDonald novels I have edited to date. Part of this may be due to MacDonald's age at the time the book was written. Though I have no way of ascertaining this, some of his linguistic powers may have been fading. I seemed to detect more frequent rambling sentences, more organizational incongruities, less vivid descriptive passages. However, none of this in any way diminished the clarity of the truths that emerged.

Adding to this challenge was the fact that I had before me two editions of the original, both first editions—one American, one British, both published in 1897, and yet *different* textually. This made it difficult to tell (something Bible translators always face) which was the "truest" mode of expression or turn of phrase according to MacDonald's mind at the time of writing. By far the majority of the sentences in each of the two books were distinct. Sometimes one seemed more clear, sometimes the other, but generally I found the British edition to be preferable; it seemed slightly more lucid, and it is my guess that it was indeed the most recent draft of the book.

Neither of MacDonald's two bibliographers (John Malcolm Bulloch, Aberdeen, 1924; and Mary Nance Jordan, Wheaton, 1984), who have extensively catalogued all known published editions of MacDonald's original works, mention this discrepency. My own conjecture is that when the book first appeared for serialization in the *Glasgow Weekly* magazine during the latter months of 1896, it was taken exactly as it was for the American edition, which was published the following year by Dodd-Mead. However, in final preparation for the British edition which was to follow the magazine's run, Mac-Donald no doubt did further editing of the manuscript. This would account for the Hurst and Blackett edition, also released in 1897, showing slightly more refinement.

One of the particular rewards in being able to share this book with you is the simple fact that this is my wife Judy's favorite of George MacDonald's novels. She has read it over and over, every time coming away with her deep hunger after God rekindled, and thirsting anew to have that purifying fire of God's love continue its surgical work in her heart.

She was quicker than I to perceive the spiritual content in *Salted With Fire*. She had read it, tearfully, three times, describing to me its impact on her, and all the while I was stalled with it. The difficulties of the original obscured for me the fundamental truths MacDonald was attempting to convey. But at every step, when I listened to what she was saying, I discovered her instincts to be true. She has always had an ear keenly tuned to MacDonald's essential themes. We all owe her our thanks for being an inspired encouragement to me, both with this book and many of the others.

Thus, this is a project which has been a double-edged labor of love on my part, both toward MacDonald, and toward her. All along I have felt as though I have been fulfilling a debt of gratitude to Judy for at last bringing into the attention of the public this book she had loved for so many years.

The novels containing Scottish dialect have been most meaningful to Judy. Somehow, the earthy and picturesque language, coming from the mouths of David Elginbrod, Andrew Comin, Janet Grant, or John MacLear, speaking in humble and simple terms about the things of God, has given the dialect itself a feel almost of holiness. To hear it in her mind's ear was to be transported to a simpler time, among simple people, who loved God with all the heart, soul, mind, and strength of their humble yet powerful lives.

Because of this it seemed only fitting to retain a good deal of that dialect while editing *Salted With Fire*. My objectives here have been just as they were in *The Laird's Inheritance*, in the Introduction to which I described the process of how and why I did what I did to the original Scots. For anyone interested I would refer you to that source, and I have here included a brief glossary for your added convenience.

For those of you interested in the man MacDonald himself, there is now available a full-length biography, entitled *George MacDonald: Scotland's Beloved Storyteller*, also published by Bethany House. It is out of the flow of the spiritual themes of his life that his books can best be understood, and it is this flow which I have tried to capture in the biography. *Salted With Fire*, especially, takes on a poignant reality in light of the later years of MacDonald's life, knowing as you read that these are among the final words for which he will be remembered.

Finally, I enjoy hearing from you. Many have written me, and both I and the publishers continue to welcome your responses. In addition to the biography, I have prepared a small pamphlet on MacDonald which I would be happy to send you upon request. I hope you will get the pamphlet, will read the biography, and will write to let us know how MacDonald has been used of the Lord in your life. God bless you all!

Michael Phillips
One Way Book Shop
1707 E Street
Eureka, CA 95501

Glossary

aboot—about
ahind—behind
ain—own
an'—and
atween—between
bed-end—inner part of house
ben—inside
bide—abide, stand
body—person
bonny—pretty
brose—oats, or oatmeal
burn—stream
canna—can't
cottar—farmer
couldna—couldn't
dautie—daughter
didna—didn't
differ—difference
dinna—don't
disna—doesn't
fer—for
gie—give
hae—have
haena—haven't
hasna—hasn't
hoo—how
jist—just
ken—know

kirk—church
kist—chest
limmer—rascal, rogue, fool
mains—farmhouse
mirk—darkness
mither—mother
muckle—much, great
nae—no
nicht—night
oot—out
o'er—over
o'—of
ony—any
sae—so
sich—such
soutar—cobbler
stourum—liquid gruel
toon—town
wee—little
weel—well
whaur—where
wi'—with
winna—won't
wi'oot—without
wouldna—wouldn't
ye—you
yer—your

1 / The Cobbler

The day would be a hot one, and the fragrant scents throughout the land had already come to life, borne on the wings of the warm morning's breezes. The subtle perfume which spoke of oats and cattle, sheep and potatoes, and greening heather, saving its explosive bloom for fall, gave the eastern Scottish countryside its essential character and its people a contentment of spirit. The night had passed, the dawn had come, and still the earth gave of itself to feed those who dwelt upon it.

Outside the rural village small farms dotted the landscape, some but an acre of rocky ground where poor cottars struggled with a cow or two and a garden of potatoes to carve out a meager living. Others, such as the holdings of Stonecross, were of considerable extent.

But size and apparent means notwithstanding, all was not as it once had been for the Blatherwicks of that estate—a family whose dawn was not yet at hand despite the coming of a new day to the land. For the son and heir of Stonecross had left home—a statement sadly reflecting truth in both the physical and spiritual realms—and within the house where hope once reigned a certain cloud of uneasiness had descended. However, the burning of liberating sorrow lying on the distant horizon was not visible to Marion and Peter Blatherwick. Their only son, James, studying in Edinburgh with hopes for the ministry, was one of whom they had been proud and for whom they had cherished dreams of a strong character. And though vague hints had grown perceptible, in their occasional disquiet they yet had little inkling to what degree he had left the home of his heavenly Father as well. Like the prodigal, but with no inheritance in hand, he had turned from both his fathers, thinking to make his mark in the world by his intellect, not his honor. But the purifying fires of his redemptive trial had not yet begun.

In God's kingdom, however, a man's salvation rarely comes without the prayers of another who labors unseen. In the village of Tiltowie, two or three miles distant, stood another house—a humble dwelling—where the householder remained in the light of loving fellowship with his Father above. John MacLear, the town's cobbler, who lived with his daughter Margaret, dwelt in a spiritual atmosphere so unlike that which surrounded young Blatherwick that few in the world—gazing upon mere appearances—would have imagined that the poor village soutar was miles farther along the road of life than the well-placed seminarian. Neither would any have guessed that the prayerful ordeal of the old man on behalf of the young childhood friend of his daughter's had been underway long before James knew there was anything within him requiring the salting of God's fire, or the prayers of a righteous man.

But though one was growing in light while the other groped in darkness, the whole story was far from told. For there is always hope even for the most wayward of God's children. The shepherd's staff of his Son never ceases seeking the lost of his father's sheep, whatever cleansing afflictions that salvation may require.

In the house of light, both old and young had risen with the sun, and now Margaret was preparing to leave her father as he glanced up from the shoes upon which his deft and careful hands had been working.

"Whaur are ye off to this bonny mornin', Maggie, my dear?" said the cobbler, looking toward his daughter as she stood in the doorway with her own shoes in her hand.

"Jist o'er t' Stonecross, wi' yer permission, Father, to ask the mistress for a few handfuls o' chaff; yer bed's grown a mite hungry for more."

"Hoot, the bed's weel enough, lassie!"

"It's anything but weel enough. 'Tis my part t' look after my ain father, an' see that there be nae knots in either his bed or his porridge."

"Ye're jist like yer mither all o'er again, lass! Weel, I winna miss ye that much, for the minister Pethrie'll be in this mornin'."

"Hoo do ye know that, Father?"

"We didna agree very weel last night, an' I'm certain he'll be back, nae jist for his shoes, but t' finish his argument."

"I canna bide that man—he's such a quarrelsome body!"

"Toots, bairn! I dinna like t' hear ye speak scornful o' the good man that has the care o' oor souls."

"It would be more t' the purpose if ye had the care o' his!"

"An' sae I have. Hasna everybody the care o' every other's?"

"Ay. But he presumes upon it—an' ye dinna; there's the difference!"

"But ye see, lassie, the man has nae insight—none t' speak o', that is. An' it's pleased God t' make him a wee bit slow an' some twisted in what he thinks. Why, we canna yet see, but 'tis for the man's own good, o' that we can be sure. He has nae notion even o' the work I put into this shoe o' his—that I'm this moment laborin' over. But his time t' see'll come. The Lord'll make sure o' that!"

"Yer work's sorely wasted on him 'at canna see the thought in it."

"Is God's work wasted upon you an' me except when we see all o' it an' understan' it, Maggie?"

The girl was silent. Her father resumed.

"There's three concerned in the matter o' the work I may be at: first, my own duty t' the work—that's me. Then him I'm workin' for—that's the minister. An' then Him that sets me t' the work—an' ye ken who that is. Noo, which o' the three would ye hae me leave oot o' the consideration?"

For another moment the girl continued silent; then she said: "Ye must be right, Father. I believe it, though I canna jist see all o' it. A body canna like everybody, an' the minister's jist the one man I canna bide."

"Ay, ye could, if ye loved the *one* as He ought t' be loved, an' as ye must learn t' love him."

"Weel, I'm not come t' that wi' the minister yet!"

"It's the truth—but 'tis a sore pity, my dautie."

"He provokes me the way he speaks to you, Father—him that's not fit t' tie the thong o' yer shoe."

"The Master would let him tie his, an' say thank ye."

"It aye seems t' me that he has such a scanty way o' believin'! It's hardly like believin' at all. He winna trust him for nothin' that he hasna his own word, or some other body's for. Do ye call that trustin' him?"

It was now the father's turn to be silent for a moment. Then he said, "Leave the judgin' o' him to his own master, lassie. I hae seen him sometimes sorely concerned fer other folk."

"Concerned that they wouldna agree wi' him, an' were condemned in consequence—wasna that it?"

"I canna answer ye that, bairn."

"Weel, I ken he doesna like you—not one wee bit. I ken he's talkin' against ye t' other folk."

"Maybe. Then more's the need I should love him."

"But hoo *can* ye, Father? The more I was t' try, the more I jist couldna."

"Ye could try, an' the Lord could help ye."

"I dinna ken. I only ken that ye say it, an' I must believe ye. None the more can I see hoo it's ever t' be brought aboot."

"No more can I, though I ken it can be. But jist think, my own Maggie, hoo would anybody else ever ken that one o' us was his disciple if we were disputin' aboot the holiest things—at least what the minister counts the holiest, though maybe I ken better? It's when two o' us strive against each other that what's called a schism begins, an' I jist winna, please God—an' it does please him. He never said, Ye must all think the same way, but he did say, Ye must all love one another, an' no strive amoong yersel's."

"Ye dinna go to his kirk, Father."

"Na, for I'm afraid sometimes lest I should stop lovin' him. It matters little aboot going t' the kirk every Sunday, but it matters a heap aboot lovin' one another."

"Weel, Father, I dinna believe that I can love him any day, so wi' yer leave, I'll be off to Stonecross afore he comes."

"Go yer way, lassie, an' the Lord go wi' ye, as once he did wi' them that was goin' t' Emmaus."

With her shoes in her hand, the girl was leaving the house when her father called after her, "Hoo'll folk ken that I provide for my own when my bairn goes unshod? If ye like, take off yer shoes when ye're oot o' the toon."

"Are ye sure there's no hypocrisy about such a false show, Father?" asked Maggie, laughing. "I must jist hide them better."

As she spoke she put them in the empty bag she carried for the chaff.

"There—that's a hidin' o' what I have—not a pretendin' t' have what I haven't! I'll be home in good time for yer tea, Father. I can walk so much better withoot them," she added as she threw the bag over her shoulder. "I'll put them on when I come t' the heather."

"Ay, ay, go yer way, an' leave me t' the work ye haena the grace t' advertise by wearin' it."

As she passed it on her way, Maggie looked in at the window and got a last sight of her father. The sun was shining into the little bare room, and her shadow fell upon him as she passed. But his form lingered clear in the chamber of her mind after she had left him far behind her. There it was not her shadow, but rather the shadow of a great peace that rested upon him as he bent over the shoe, his mind fixed indeed upon his work, but far more occupied with the affairs of quite another region.

Mind and soul were each so absorbed in their accustomed labor that never did either interfere with that of the other. His shoemaking lost nothing when he was deepest sunk in some one or other of the words of his Lord which he was seeking to understand. In his leisure hours he was an intense reader, but it was nothing in any book that now occupied him; it was instead the live good news, the man Jesus Christ himself. In thought, in love, in imagination, that man dwelt in him, was alive in him, and made him alive. For the cobbler believed absolutely in the Lord of Life, was always trying to do the things he said, and to keep his words abiding in him. Therefore he was what the parson called a mystic, yet was at the same time the most practical man in the neighborhood. Therefore, he made the best shoes, because the work of the Lord did abide in him.

Not many more minutes passed when the door opened and the minister came into the kitchen. The cobbler always worked there that he might be near his daughter, whose presence never interrupted neither his work or his thought, or even his prayers, which at times seemed involuntary as a vital automatic impulse.

"It's a grand day," said the minister. "It seems to me that on just such a day will the Lord come, nobody expecting him, and the folk all following their various callings, just as when the flood came and surprised them all.''

Without realizing it, the man was reflecting on what the soutar had been saying during their previous discussion. Neither did he happen to think, at the moment, that it was the Lord himself who had said it first.

"An' I was thinkin', this very minute,'' returned the cobbler, "that it would be a bonny day for the Lord t' go aboot among his own folk. I was thinkin' that maybe he was walkin' wi' Maggie up the hill t' Stonecross—closer t' her, maybe, than she could see or think.''

"You're a good deal taken up with vain imaginings, MacLear,'' returned the minister. "What scripture do you have for such a notion, that has no practical value?''

"Indeed, sir, what scripture hae I for takin' my breakfast on this or any mornin'? Yet I ne'er look for a judgment t' fall upon me for eatin' it! I think we do more things in faith than we ken—yet still not enough! I was thankful for what I ate, though, I know that, an' maybe that'll stan' for faith. But if I go on this way, we'll be beginnin' as we left off last night! An' we hae t' love one anither, not accordin' t' what the one thinks, but accordin' as each kens the Master loves the other, for he loves the two o' us t'gither.''

"But how do you know he's pleased with you?''

"I said nothin' aboot that. I said he loves us.''

"For that he must be pleased with you.''

"I dinna think aboot that. I jist take my life in my han', an' give it t' him. An' he's ne'er turned his face from me yet. Eh, sir! think what it would be if he did!''

"But we mustn't think of him other than he would have us think.''

"That's why I'm hangin' aroun' his door, an' lookin' aboot for him.''

"Well, I don't know what to make of you. I must just leave you to him.''

"Ye couldna do a kinder thing! I desire nothin' better from man or minister than t' be left t' him.''

"Well, well, see to yourself.''

"I'll see t' him, an' try t' love my neighbor—that's you, Mr. Pethrie. I'll hae yer shoes ready by Saturday. I trust they'll be worthy o' the feet God made, an' that hae t' be shod by me. I trust an' believe they'll not distress ye, or interfere wi' yer preachin'. I'll bring them to ye mysel'."

"No, no, don't do that! Let Maggie come with them. You would only be putting me out of humor for the Lord's work with your foolish carrying on."

"Weel, I'll sen' Maggie, then—only ye might oblige me by not talkin' t' her, for ye might put *her* oot o' humor, an' then she mightna give yer sermon fair play the mext mornin'."

The minister closed the door with some sharpness.

2 / The Student

In the meantime Maggie was walking shoeless and bonnetless up the hill to the farm she sought. The June morning was now hot, tempered by a wind from the northwest. The land was green with the slow-rising tide of the young grain, among which the cool wind made little waves, showing the brown earth between them on the dry face of the hill. A few fleecy clouds shared the high blue realm with the keen sun.

As she rose to the top of the road, the gable of the house came suddenly into her sight, and near it was a sleepy old gray horse, treading his ceaseless round at the end of a long lever, too listless to feel the weariness of a labor that to him must have seemed unprogressive. It did not seem to give the horse any consolation to listen to the commotion he was causing on the other side of the wall, where an antiquated threshing machine was in full response with many diverse movements to the monotony of his circular motion. Nearby a peacock, as conscious of his glorious plumage as indifferent to the ugliness of his feet, kept time with his swaying neck to the motion of those same feet, as he strode with stagey gait across the cornyard, now and then stooping to spitefully pick up a stray grain, and occasionally erecting his neck to give utterance to a hideous cry of satisfaction at his own beauty, as unlike it as ever discord was to harmony.

Just as the sun touched the meridian the old horse stopped and stood still; the hour of rest and food had come, and he knew it. The girl passed one of the green-painted doors of the farmhouse and stopped at the kitchen one. It stood open, and a ruddy maid answered her knock, with question in her eyes and a smile on her lips at sight of the shoemaker's daughter, whom she knew well. Maggie asked if she might see the mistress.

"Here's the soutar's Maggie wantin' ye, mem!" called the maid, and Mrs. Blatherwick, who was close at hand, came forward and

Maggie humbly but confidently made her request. It was kindly granted, and Maggie at once proceeded to the barn to fill the bag she had brought with the light plumy covering of the husk of the oats, the mistress of Stonecross helping her, and talking away to her as she did so, for both the soutar and his daughter were favorites with her and her husband, and she had not seen either of them for some time.

"Ye used t' know oor James in the old days, Maggie," she went on, for the two had played together as children at school, although growth and difference of station had gradually put an end to their friendship. As much as she liked Maggie, the mother now referred to her son somewhat guardedly, seeing that James was now on his way to becoming a great man since he was a divinity student. For in the Scotch church every minister, until he has discredited himself at least, is regarded with quite a high degree of respect, and therefore her son was prospectively to his mother a man of no little note.

Maggie remembered how, when a boy, he had liked to talk to her father, who listened to him with a curious look on his rugged face, while he set forth the commonplaces of a lifeless theology. But she remembered also that she had never heard her father make the slightest attempt to lay open to the youth his stores of what one or two in the place counted wisdom and knowledge. He only listened, and, until young James should ask for his insight, seemed content to say little on his own side.

"He's a clever laddie," he had once said to Maggie, "an' if he gets his eyes open in the course o' his life, he'll doubtless see somethin'. But he disna yet ken that there's anything real t' be seen ootside or inside o' him." When he heard that he was going to study divinity, he shook his head and was silent.

"I'm jist home from payin' him a short visit," Mrs. Blatherwick went on. "I came home but two nights ago. He's lodgin' wi' a decent widow in Arthur Street, in a room up a long stair. She looks after his clothes an' sees t' the washin' an' does her best t' keep him tidy. But Jeamie was always particular aboot his appearance! So I was weel pleased wi' the old woman."

The conversation gradually moved into other channels until Maggie's bag was full, and with hearty thanks she took her leave of Mrs. Blatherwick and returned to her father, to whom she passed on the news of James she had received. The cobbler received it with a somber expression, turned away from his work for a few moments, and was silent. Maggie always knew when he was praying, and left him alone. She did not altogether understand the deep concern he had shown of late for the young Blatherwick, but she respected it because she knew it originated out of his heart of compassion.

In her conveyance of the news concerning her son, however, Mrs. Blatherwick did not open the discussion in the direction that should have been of most concern. For there was another in the Edinburgh lodging who did not appear more often than she must, at least so long as Mrs. Blatherwick was there, and of whom the mother had made no mention to her husband upon her return, any more than she did on this day to Maggie MacLear. Indeed, at first she had taken so little notice of her that she could hardly be said to have seen her at all.

This was a girl of about sixteen, who did far more for the comfort of her aunt's two lodgers than her aunt who reaped all the advantage. If Mrs. Blatherwick had let her eyes rest upon her but for a moment, she would probably have looked again, and would certainly have discovered that she was a good-looking and graceful little creature, with blue eyes and hair as black and fine and plentiful as could be imagined. She might have discovered as well a certain look of devotion which, when it came to her relation to her son James, Mrs. Blatherwick would assuredly have counted dangerous. But seeing her poorly dressed and looking untidy, the mother took her for an ordinary servant girl and gave her no particular attention. And she did not for a moment doubt that her son saw the girl just as she did.

He was her only son, and her heart was full of ambition for him, and she thought long about the honor he would eventually bring her and his father. The father, however, caring much less for his good looks, had neither the same satisfaction in him nor an equal expectation from him. In fact, neither of his parents had as yet reaped much pleasure from his existence, however full their hopes might be for the time to come. There were two things working against such parental satisfaction—the first, that James had never been open-hearted and communicative of his feelings or doings toward them; and the second, and the worse, he had come to feel a certain unexpressed claim of superiority over them. It would surely have done nothing to comfort their uneasiness about him had they noted that the existence of such a feeling of superiority was more or less evident in all his relationships with most everyone he met. This conceit showed itself in a stiff incommunicative reluctance, a contempt for any sort of manual labor, by the affectation of a ridiculously proper form of English, from all of which his simple and old-fashioned father shrank with dislike.

He was glad enough that his son should be better educated than himself, but he could not help feeling that his son's ways of asserting himself were but signs of foolishness, especially as conjoined with his wish to be a minister. Peter was full of simple paternal affection, yet it was completely quenched by the behavior of his son. He was continually aware of something that seemed an impassable gulf between his son and his parents. Peter himself was profoundly religious and full of a great and simple righteousness—that is, of a loving sense of fair play, a very different thing, indeed, from what most of those who count themselves religious mean when they talk of the righteousness of God.

However, James was little able to yet see this or other great qualities in his father. It was not that he was consciously disrespectful to either of his parents, or even that his behavior was unloving. He honored their character, but shrank from the simplicity of their manners. He had never been disobedient and had done what he could to be outwardly religious enough to convince himself that he was a righteous youth, or at least enough to nourish his ignorance of the fact that he was far from being the person of moral strength that he imagined himself. The person he saw in the mirror of his self-consciousness was a very fine and altogether trustworthy young man; the reality so twisted in its reflection was but a decent lad, as lads go, who had not the slightest notion of his true self.

James was one of the many bound up in the slavery of reverencing the judgments of society. Often without knowing it, such judge life, and truth itself, by the falsest of all measures—that is, the judgment of others falser than themselves. They do not ask what is true or right, but what folk will think and say about this or that. James, for instance, completely missed the point of what being a gentleman was, but his habit was of always asking, in such and such a circumstance, how a gentleman would behave. Thinking himself a man of honor, he would never tell a lie or break a promise. But he did not mind raising expectations that he had not the least intention of fulfilling, a more subtle misapplication of the same virtue.

Being a Scot lad, it is hardly to be wondered at that he should turn to theology as a means of livelihood. Neither is it surprising that he should have done so without any conscious love for God, for it is not in Scotland alone that men take refuge in the church when they have no genuine call to it. James's ambition was nonetheless contemptible that it was a common one—that, namely, of distinguishing himself in the pulpit.

Mr. Pethrie, the local minister whom it cost the cobbler so much care and effort to love, was yet far removed from James in this regard. Personal ambition did not count a great deal with him, which surely one day would be counted to his credit. Though intellectually small, he was a good man and certainly not a coward where he judged people's souls in danger. He sought to save the world by preaching a God eminently respectable to those who could believe in such a God, even though the God he preached was not a particularly grand one. Through his life, nevertheless, he showed himself in many ways a believer in him who revealed a grand and larger God indeed— which did not, however, prevent him from looking down on the cobbler as one whose notions were in rebellion against God.

But young Blatherwick was cut out of a different cloth even than old and good Mr. Pethrie. He had already, as a result of his theological studies, begun to turn his back upon several of the special tenets of Calvinism. This in itself, of course, made of him neither a better nor a worse man. He had cast aside, for instance, the doctrine of an everlasting hell for the unbeliever. But in so doing, as with other doctrines, he did not fill himself instead with a heart after truth and a love for the Man of Truth, but left his fields fallow for the cultivation of nothing but weeds and half-baked notions of men. Sweeping his empty house clean, he made of it all the more suitable a home for the demons of falsehood because he did not seek doctrines of truth with which to replace those he repudiated.

Mr. Pethrie, on the other hand, held to the aforementioned doctrine as absolutely fundamental, as with all those of Scottish Calvinism, while the cobbler, who had discarded it almost from his childhood, positively refused to enter into any argument on the matter with the disputatious little man. Long ago he had learned that the minister was unable to perceive any force in his argument that to tell a man he *must* one day give in and repent would have greater force with the unbeliever than to tell him that the hour would come when repentance itself would do no good.

In the meantime, as James studied his Scotch theology, he kept his changing views to himself. He knew the success of his probation and ministerial license depended on his skillfully concealing any hint of his freer opinions. He must not jeopardize his career until his position was secure.

He was in his final year, and the close of his studies in divinity was drawing close at hand.

3 / The Sin

The day was a stormy one in the great northern city, and young James Blatherwick sat in the same shabbily furnished room where his mother had visited him in the ancient house, preparing for what he regarded as his career. The great clock of a church in the neighboring street had just begun to strike five of a wintry afternoon, dark with snow—falling and still to fall—when a gentle tap came to his door. He opened it to the same girl I have already mentioned, who came in with a tray and the makings for his most welcomed meal of coffee and bread and butter. She set it down in silence, which seemed to contain more than the mere silence of a servant, gave him one glance of devotion, and was turning to leave the room when he looked up from the paper he was writing, and said, "Don't be in such a hurry, Isy. Haven't you time to pour out my coffee for me?"

Isy was a small, dark, neat little girl, with finely formed features, and a look of childlike simplicity, not altogether different from childlikeness. She answered him first with her blue eyes full of love and trust, and then with her voice.

"Plenty of time. What else do I have to do than to see you're comfortable?"

He shoved aside his work, looked up at her with some intent consideration in his gaze, pushed his chair back a little from the table, and replied, "What's the matter with you this last day or two, Isy? You've not been like yourself."

She hesitated a moment, then answered, "It's nothing, I suppose, but just that I'm growing older and beginning to think about things."

She stood near him. He put his arm round her little waist and tried to draw her down to sit upon his knees, but she resisted.

"I don't see what difference that can make all at once, Isy. We've known each other so long there can be no misunderstanding between us. You have always been good and modest, and most attentive to me all the time I have been in your aunt's house."

"That's but been my duty. But it's almost over now!" she said with a sigh that indicated tears somewhere, and yielded to the increased pressure of his arm.

"What makes you say that?" he returned, giving her a warm kiss, plainly neither unwelcome nor the first.

"Don't you think it would be better to drop that kind of thing now?" she said, and tried to rise from his lap, but he held her fast.

"Why now, more than at any other time? What is the difference with today all of a sudden? What has put this idea into your pretty little head?" he asked.

"It has to come someday, and the longer from now the harder it'll be."

"But tell me, what has set you to thinking about it all at once?"

She burst into tears. He tried to soothe and comfort her, but in struggling not to cry she only sobbed the worse. At last, however, she succeeded in faltering out an explanation.

"Auntie's been telling me that I should look after my heart so I won't lose it altogether! But it's gone already," she went on with a fresh outburst; "and it's no use crying to it to come back to me! I might as well cry on the wind as it blows by me. I can't understand it. I know well enough you'll soon be a great man with all the town wanting to hear you. And I know just as well that I'll have to sit still in my seat and look up to where you stand—not daring to say a word, not even daring to think a thought lest somebody sitting beside me should hear what I'm thinking. For it would be impudent then for me to think that once I was sitting where I'm sitting now—and right in the very church."

"Didn't you ever think, Isy, that maybe I might marry you someday?" said James jokingly, confident in the social gulf between them.

"No, not once. I knew better than that! I never even wished it. For that would be no friend's wish; you would never get on if you did. I'm not fit to be a minister's wife—nor worthy of it. I might not do that badly in a tiny little place—but among grand folk, in a big town—for that's where you're sure to be—eh me, me! All the last week or two I haven't been able to help seeing you drifting away from me, out and out to the great sea where never a thought of Isy would come near you again; and why should there? You didn't come into the world to think about me or the likes of me, but to be a great preacher and leave me behind you, like a sheaf of corn you have just cut and left in the field!"

Here came another burst of bitter weeping, followed by words whose very articulation was a succession of sobs.

"Eh me! Now I've clean disgraced myself!"

As to young Blatherwick, I doubt that anything of evil intent was passing through his mind during this confession, and yet what was it but utterly selfish that he found a certain gratification in the fact that this simplehearted and very pretty girl loved him unsought, and had told him unasked? A truehearted man would have at once perceived what he was bringing upon her and taken steps to stop it. But James's vanity got the upper hand over him. And while his ambition made him think of himself as so much her superior that there could be no thought of marrying her, it did not prevent him from yielding to the delight of being so admired. Isy left the room not a little consoled and with a new hope in her innocent imagination. James remained to exult over his conquest and indulge a more definite pleasure than before in the person and devotion of the girl. As to any consciousness of danger to either of them, it was no more than the uneasy stir on the shore of a storm far out at sea.

As to her fitness to be a minister's wife, he had never asked himself a question concerning it. But in truth, she could very soon have grown far fitter for the position than he was now for that of a minister. In character she was much beyond him, and in breeding and consciousness far more of a lady than he of a gentleman. Her manners were immeasurably better than his, because they were simple and aimed at nothing; she had no hidden motives. Instinctively she avoided anything she would have recognized as uncomely. She did not know that simplicity was the purest breeding, yet from mere truth of nature practiced it without knowing it. If her words were old-fashioned, her tone was less so. James would, I am sure, have admired her if she had been dressed on Sundays in something more showy than a simple cotton gown. But her aunt was poor, and she even poorer, for she had no fixed wages. And I fear that her poverty had its influence in the freedoms he allowed himself with her.

Isy's aunt was a weak as well as unsuspicious woman, who had known better days, and pitied herself because they were past and gone. She gave herself no anxiety about her niece's prudence. It would have required a man, not merely of greater goodness than James, but of greater insight into the realities of life as well, to perceive the worth of the girl who waited upon him with a devotion far more angelic than servile.

Thus things went on for a while, with a continuous strengthening of the pleasant yet not altogether easy bonds in which Isobel walked, and a constant increase in the power of the attraction that drew the student to the self-yielding girl. At last the appearance of another lodger in the house, with the necessary attentions he began to demand as well on Isy's time, was the means of opening young Blatherwick's eyes to the state of his own feelings. Realizing that he was dangerously in peril of falling in love with one of such low station, he knew that if he did not mean to go further, here it must stop. He therefore began to change a little in his behavior toward her whenever she came into his room to serve him.

Poor Isy was immediately aware of the change but attributed it to a temporary absorption in his studies. Soon, however, she could not doubt that not merely was his voice changed toward her, but that his heart had also grown cold to her. For there was more at work than mere jealousy; what concerned the minister-to-be more than anything was the danger into which he was drifting of irrecoverably damaging his prospects for the future with an imprudent marriage. "To be saddled with a wife," as he expressed it to himself, before he had the opportunity to distinguish himself and before a church was attainable to him was a thing he could not contemplate even for a moment. So when one day Isobel sorrowfully asked him some indifferent question, the uneasy knowledge that he was on the verge of wrecking her happiness all the more by his rejection made him answer her roughly. White as a ghost she stood silently staring at him for a moment, sick at heart, and then fainted on the floor.

He was suddenly seized with an overpowering remorse that brought back all the tenderness he had felt for her earlier. James sprang to her, lifted her in his arms, laid her on the sofa, and cast all his previous cautions to the wind by lavishing caresses and kisses upon her, until she recovered sufficiently to know that she lay in the false paradise of his arms, while he knelt over her in a passion of regret, the first such passion of love he had felt for her. He poured into her ear words of incoherent dismay, which, taking shape as she revived, soon became promises of love and vows to remain with her forever. Thereupon, worse consequences followed. Dreamily coming to herself, before she was fully master of her emotions again, Isy returned his affections heatedly, with the result that her fervid lover lost control of his altogether. At the moment when self-restraint had become most imperative, his trust in his own honor became the last loop of the snare about to entangle his and her very life. At the moment when a genuine love would have stopped, in order to surround her with arms of safety rather than passion, he ceased to be his sister's keeper. Cain ceased to be his brother's when he slew him.

But the vengeance on his unpremeditated treachery came close upon its heels. The moment Isy left the room weeping and pallid, conscious of no love but rather of a miserable shame. James threw himself down, writhing as in the claws of a hundred demons. He had done the unthinkable!

And the day after the next he was to preach his first sermon in front of his class, in the presence of his professor of divinity! His immediate impulse was to rush from the house and home to his mother on foot. It would probably have been well for him had he indeed done so, confessed everything, and turned his back on the church and his paltry ambition altogether. But he had never been open with his mother, and he feared his father, not knowing the tender righteousness of his heart, or the springs of love that would at once have opened to meet the sorrowful tale of his sliding-back son.

But instead of fleeing at once to that city of refuge, he fell to pacing the room in helpless bewilderment. And it was not long before he was searching every corner of his reviving consciousness—not exactly for any justification, but for what rationalization of his "fault" might be found. And it was not long before a multitude of sneaking arguments, imps of Satan, began to come at the cry of the agony of this lover of self.

But in that agony there came no detestation of himself because of his humiliation of the trusting Isobel. He did not yet loathe his abuse of her confidence by his miserable weakness—the hour of a true and good repentance was not yet come. The only shame he felt was in the failure of his own fancied strength; there was as yet no shame in the realization of what he was. All he could think of was what contempt would come to him if the thing should ever come to be known. The pulpit, the goal of his ambition, the field of his imagined triumphs, the praise he had dreamed of all these years— had he thrown it all away in a moment of folly? The very thought of it made him sick!

Still, there yet lay the chance that no one might hear a word of what had happened. Isy would surely never tell anyone—least of all her aunt! He had promised to marry the poor girl, and that possibly he would have to do. But it could be managed, though certainly nothing was to be contemplated any time soon. There could at the moment be no necessity for such an extreme measure.

He would wait and see. He would be guided by events. As to the sin of the act—how many countless others had fallen like him, and no one had ever been the wiser! Never would he so offend womankind again. And in the meantime, he would let it go, and try to forget it— in the hope that Providence now, and at some future time, would bury it from all men's sight. He would go on the same as if the ugly thing had not so cruelly happened, had cast no such cloud over the fair future that lay before him.

And by the time his rationalizations had progressed this far, they had—as they often do—become justifications, and his selfish regrets came to be mingled with a certain annoyance that Isy should have yielded so easily. Why had she not aided him to resist the weakness that had wrought his undoing? She was as much to blame as he. And for her unworthiness was he to be left to suffer?

Within half an hour he had returned to the sermon he had in hand, revising it for the twentieth time, to have it perfect before finally committing it to memory; for the orator would have it seem the very thing it was not—the outcome of extemporaneous feeling—so the lie of his life be crowned with success. During what remained of the next two days he spared no labor, and at last delivered it with considerable unction and felt he had achieved his end. On neither of those days did Isy make any appearance. Her aunt told him that she was in bed with a bad headache.

The next day she was about her work as usual, but never once looked up. He imagined that she was mad at him and did not venture to say a word. But indeed, he had no wish to speak to her, for what was there to be said? A cloud was between them; a great gulf seemed to divide them. He found he was no longer attracted to her, and wondered how he could have so delighted in her presence only a short while earlier.

It was not that his resolve to marry her wavered; he fully intended to keep his promise to her. But he would have to wait for the proper time, the right opportunity to reveal his engagement to his parents. But after a few days, during which there had been no return to their former familiarity, it was with a fearful kind of relief that he learned she was gone to pay a visit to an old grandmother in the country. He did not care that she had gone without saying goodbye to him; he only wondered if she could have said anything to incriminate him. The school session came to an end while she was still gone. He formally moved out of her aunt's house, and went home to Stone-cross.

His father at once felt a wider division between them than before, and his mother was now compelled also to acknowledge that they were not one with their son. At the same time he carried himself with less arrogance, and seemed almost humbled rather than uplifted by his success with his schooling.

During the year that followed he made several visits to Edinburgh, but never did he inquire or hear anything about Isy. Before long he received a position in a somewhat stylish parish, by way of a gift from a certain duke who had always been friendly with his father as an unassuming tenant of one of his largest farms in the north. With a benefice in hand whereby he could put to use his less than modest ecclesiastical gifts, he might now have taken steps to fulfill his promises to Isy. But even then he could not quite persuade himself that the right time had come for revealing it to his parents. He knew it would be a great blow to his mother to learn he had so handicapped his future, and he feared the silent face of his father listening to the announcement of it.

It is hardly necessary to say that he made no attempt to establish any correspondence with the poor girl. But this time he was not unwilling to forget her, and found himself hoping that she had, if not forgotten, at least dismissed from her mind all that had taken place between them. Now and then in the night he would have a few tender thoughts about her, but in the morning they would all be gone, and he would drown painful reminiscence in the care with which he would polish and repolish his sentences, trying to imitate the style of the great orators of the day. Apparent richness of composition was his principal aim, not truth of meaning or clarity of utterance.

I can hardly be presumptuous in adding that, although thus growing in a certain popularity, he was not growing in favor with God, for who can that makes the favor of man his aim? And as he continued to hear nothing about Isy, the hope at length awoke in him, bringing with it a keen shot of pleasure, that he was never to hear any more of her. For the praise of men, and the love of that praise, had now restored him to his own good graces, and he thought more highly of himself than ever. His continued lack of inquiry about her, despite the predicament in which he might possibly have placed her in, was a worse sin, being deliberate, than his primary wrong to her. And it was that which now recoiled upon him in his increase of hardness and self-satisfaction.

He had not been in his parish more than a month or two when he was attracted by a certain young woman in his congregation. She was of some inborn refinement and distinction of position, and he quickly became anxious to win her approval, and, if possible, her admiration.

So in preaching—if the word used for the lofty utterance of divine messengers may be misapplied to his paltry memorizations—his main thought was always whether she was justly appreciating the eloquence and wisdom with which he meant to impress her. Even though her deep natural insight penetrated him and his pretensions, in truth she encouraged him, thus making him all the more eager after her good opinion. He came at last to imagine himself thoroughly in love with her—a thing at present impossible to him with any woman.

Finally, encouraged by the fancied importance of his position, and his own fancied distinction in it, he ventured an offer of his feeble hand and feebler heart—only to have them, to his surprise, definitely and absolutely refused. He turned from her door a good deal disappointed, but severely mortified. And judging it impossible for any woman to keep silence concerning such a refusal, and unable to endure the thought of the gossip that would come of it and to be the object of what snickers would inevitably follow, he began at once to look about for some place to hide. Very frankly, he told his patron the whole story.

It happened to suit the duke's plans, and he speedily came to his assistance with the offer of his native parish. From that post the cobbler's argumentative friend, Mr. Pethrie, had recently been elevated to a position, probably not a very distinguished one, in the kingdom of heaven. Thus, it seemed a thing most natural, and even rather pious, when James Blatherwick exchanged his parish to become minister in the one where he was born, and where his father and mother continued to occupy the old farm of Stonecross.

4 / The Daughter

The village soutar John MacLear was still meditating on spiritual things, still reading the Gospels, still making and mending shoes, and still watching the development of his daughter. She had now unfolded into what many of the neighbors counted nothing less than beauty. The farm laborers in the vicinity were nearly all more or less her admirers, and many a pair of shoes was carried to her father for the sake of a possible smile from Maggie. But a certain awe of her kept them from presuming beyond a word of greeting or farewell. Her dark and in a way mysterious look had a great deal to do with it, for it seemed to suggest behind it a beauty her face itself was unable to reveal.

She was a little short in stature, being of a strong active type, well proportioned, with a calm and clear face, and quiet but keen dark eyes. Her complexion owed its white rose tinge to a strong but gentle life, and its few freckles to the pale sun of Scotland and the breezes she met bonnetless on the hills when she accompanied her father on his walks, or when she delivered some piece of work he had finished.

Her father rejoiced in her delight with the wind, thinking that it indicated a sympathy with the Spirit whose symbol it was. He loved to think of that Spirit folding her about, closer and more lovingly than his own soul.

Almost from the moment of her mother's death, she had given herself to his service, first in doing all the little duties of the house, and then, as her strength and abilities grew, in helping him more and more in his trade. By degrees she had grown so familiar with the lighter parts of it that he could leave them to her with confidence. As soon as she had cleared away the few things necessary for their breakfast of porridge and milk, Maggie would hasten to join her father stooping over his workbench, for he was a little near-sighted.

When he lifted his head you might see that, despite the ruggedness of his face, he was a good-looking man, with strong, well-proportioned features, in which, even on Sundays, when he scrubbed his face unmercifully, there would still remain lines suggestive of ingrained rosin and heelball. On weekdays he was not so careful to remove every sign of the labor by which he earned his bread, but when his work was over till the morning, and he was free to sit down to a book, he would never even touch one without first carefully washing his hands and face.

In the workshop Maggie's place was a leather-seated stool like her father's, a yard or so away from his, to leave room for his elbows in drawing out the rosined threads as he sewed his work. There every morning she would resume whatever work she had left unfinished the night before. It was a curious trait in the father, inherited at an early age by the daughter, that he would never rise from a finished job, however near it might be quitting time, without having begun another one to go on with in the morning. Thus he kept himself from wasting time as so many unproductive persons do "between jobs." Always moving directly from one to another, he found himself ready each morning to take right up where he left off with no loss of momentum. It was wonderful how much cleaner Maggie managed to keep her hands. But then to her naturally fell the lighter work. She declared herself ambitious, however, of one day making a perfect pair of top boots with her own hands, from top to bottom.

The advantages she gained from this constant interaction with her father were incalculable. To the great benefit and rapid development of her freedom of thought, the soutar would avoid no subject as unsuitable for the girl's consideration, insisting only on its being regarded from the highest attainable point of view. Matters of little or no significance they seldom, if ever, discussed. Though she was full of an honest hilarity that was ever ready to break out when occasion occurred, she was at the same time incapable of a light word upon a sacred subject. Very early in life she became aware of the kind of joke her father would take or refuse. The light use especially of any word of the Lord would sink him in a profound silence. If it were an ordinary man who had said it, he might rebuke him by asking if he remembered who said those words. But if it was a clergyman who thus spoke lightly, MacLear was likely to respond more strongly.

Indeed the most powerful force in Maggie's education was the evident attitude of her father toward the Son of Man. Around the name of Jesus gathered his whole consciousness and hope of well-being. And it was hardly surprising that certain of his ways of thinking should pass into the mind of his child, and there show themselves as original and necessary truths. Mingling with her delight in the inanimate powers of nature, in the sun and the wind, in the rain and the growth, in the running waters and the darkness sown with stars, was such a sense of the presence of God that she felt he might appear at any moment to her or her father.

Two or three miles away, in the heart of the hills, on the outskirts of the farm of Stonecross, lived an old cottar and his wife, who paid a few shillings of rent to Mr. Blatherwick for the acre or two their ancestors had redeemed from the heather and bog. Their one son remained at home with them, and they gave occasional service on the farm when needed. They were much respected by both Peter and Marion Blatherwick, as well as by the small circle to which they were known in the neighboring village of Tiltowie—better known and more respected still in that region called the kingdom of heaven. For they were such as he to whom the promise was given that he should see the angels ascending and descending on the Son of Man. They had been close to the cobbler for many years and had long heartily loved and respected him, since even before the death of his wife. They could not exactly pity the motherless Maggie, seeing she had such a father, yet they lost no opportunity to befriend her. For old Eppie Cormack especially had occasional moments of anxiety as to how the soutar's bairn would grow up without a mother's care. No sooner, however, did the character of the little one begin to show itself, than Eppie's worries began to lessen; and long before the present time the child and the childlike old woman were fast friends. For this reason Maggie was often invited to spend a day at their home at Bogsheuch—oftener in fact than she felt a liberty to leave her father and their work in the shop, though not oftener than she would have liked to go.

One morning early in the summer, when first the hillsides had begun to look attractive, a small wooden agricultural cart, such as is now but seldom seen, with little paint left except on its two red wheels, and drawn by a thin, long-haired horse, stopped at the door of the soutar's house—clay-floored and straw-thatched, in a back lane of the village. It was a cart Mr. Cormack used in the cultivation of his little holding, and his son who was now driving it—now nearly middle-aged himself—was likely to succeed to the hut and acres of Bogsheuch, and continue the little farming they were able to do long after his father had laid his tools down in exchange for his rest. Man and cart and horse were all well known to the soutar and Maggie, and on this particular day they had come with an invitation, more pressing than usual, to pay them a visit.

Father and daughter consulted together and arrived at the conclusion that she should go with Andrew; work was more slack than usual, and nobody was in need of a promised job that the cobbler could not finish by himself in good time. Despite a slight pang at the thought of leaving her father alone, Maggie jumped up joyfully and set about preparing their dinner. In the meantime, Andrew went to carry out a few items of business that the mistress at Stonecross and his mother at Bogsheuch had given him. By the time he returned, MacLear and his daughter were just finishing their humble dinner, and Maggie was in her Sunday dress, with her week-day things and a petticoat in a bundle, for she hoped to be of some use to Eppie with the work during her visit.

Andrew brought the cart to the door, and Maggie scrambled into it.

"Take a piece wi' ye," said her father, following her to the cart. "Ye hadna muckle dinner, an' ye may be hungry again afore ye hae the long road ahind ye!"

He put several pieces of oatcake in her hand, which she took with a loving smile. They set out at a walking pace, which Andrew made no attempt to quicken.

It was far from a comfortable carriage, and there was not so much as a wisp of straw in the bottom of it for her to sit on. But the change to the out-of-doors from the close attention to her work—the open air on her face and the free rush of the thoughts that came crowding into her brain—at once put her in a blissful mood. Even the few dull remarks that the slow-thinking Andrew made at intervals from his perch on the front of the cart seemed to come to her from the mysterious world that lay in the fairy-like folds of the huddled hills about them. Everything Maggie saw or heard that afternoon seemed to wear the glamour of God's imagination, which is at once the birth and the very truth of everything. Selfishness alone can rub away that divine gilding, without which gold itself is poor indeed.

Suddenly the little horse came to a stop and stood still. Waking up from a snooze, Andrew at once jumped to the ground, and still half asleep began to search about for the cause of the sudden stop. Jess, the old horse, though she could not make haste, never had been known to stand still while still able to walk. On her part, however, Maggie had for sometime noted that they were making very slow progress.

"She's a dead cripple!" said Andrew at length, straightening his long back after an examination of Jess's forefeet. He came to Maggie's side of the cart with a serious face. "I dinna believe the creature can gae one step further. Yet I canna see what's happened t' her!"

Maggie jumped out of the cart, and again Andrew attempted to lead the horse by the rein. But it was immediately clear the animal was in pain.

"It would be cruelty!" he said. "We must jist loose her, an' take her if we can t' the How o' the Mains. They'll gie her a nicht's quarters there, poor thing! An' we'll see if they can tak ye in as weel, Maggie. The maister'll len' me a horse t' come fer ye in the mornin'."

"I winna hear o' it!" answered Maggie. "I can tramp the rest o' the way as weel's you, Andrew!"

"But I hae the things t' carry, an' that'll lea' me no han' t' help ye ower the burn!" he objected.

"What!" she returned. "I was sae tired o' sittin' that my legs are jist like t' rin awa' wi' me. Here, gie me that loaf. I'll carry that, an' my ain bit bundle as weel; then, I fancy, ye can manage the rest yersel'!"

Andrew never had a great deal to say, and against such a determined and quick thinking young lass as Maggie, by now he had nothing. But her readiness relieved him of some anxiety, for he knew his mother would be very uncomfortable if he went home without her.

The darkness gradually came on, and as it deepened Maggie's

spirits rose. And the wind became to her a live shadow, in which—
with no eye-boundaries to the space enclosing her—she could go on
imagining according to the freedom of her own wild will. As the
world and everything in it disappeared, it grew easier to imagine
Jesus making the darkness light about him, and then stepping from
it plain before her sight. That could be no trouble to him, she told
herself. Since he was everywhere, he must be there. If she were but
fit to see him, then surely he would come to her.

Her father had several times spoken in such a manner to her,
talking about the various appearances of the Lord after his resurrection, and his promise that he would be with his disciples always to
the end of the world. Even after he had gone back to his Father, had
he not appeared to the Apostle Paul? Might it not be that he had
shown himself to many another through the long ages?

In any case, he was everywhere, she thought, and always about
them, although now, perhaps from lack of faith in the earth, he had
not been seen for a long time. And she remembered her father once
saying that nobody could even *think* a thing if there was no possible
truth in it. The Lord went away that they might believe in him when
they could not see him, and so they would be in him, and he in them!

"I dinna think," said Maggie to herself, as she trudged along
beside the delightfully silent Andrew, "that my father would be the
least astonished—only filled wi' an awful gladness—if at some moment, walkin' by his side, the Lord was to call him by his name and
appear t' him. He would but think he had jist stepped oot upon him
frae some secret door, an' would say, 'I thoucht I would see ye
someday, Lord! I was aye longin' efter a sicht o' ye, Lord, an' here
ye are!' "

5 / The Baby

As they walked silently along, Maggie's thoughts on the Lord, all at once the cry of an infant came through the dark. Maggie's first thought was of the Lord when he first appeared on earth as a baby.

She stopped in the dusky starlight, and listened with her very soul.

"Andrew!" she said, for she heard the sound of his steps continuing on in front of her, though she could but vaguely see him, "Andrew, what was yon cry?"

"I heard nothin'," answered Andrew, stopping and listening.

Then came a second cry, a feeble, sad wail, and this time both of them heard it.

Maggie darted off in the direction where it seemed to come from, and she did not have far to run, for the tiny voice could hardly have reached any great distance.

They had been climbing a dreary, desolate ridge where the road was a mere stony hollow, in winter a path for the rain rather than the feet of men. On each side of it lay a wild moor covered with heather and low berry-bearing shrubs. Under a big bush Maggie saw something glimmer. She flew toward it, and found a child. It might have been a year old, but was so small and poorly nourished that its age was hard to guess.

With the instinct of a mother, she caught it up and clasped it close to her panting chest. She was delighted to find its crying cease the moment it felt her arms about it. Andrew had dropped the things he had been carrying, and had started after her, and now met her halfway back to the road, so absorbed in her newfound treasure that she scarcely noticed him. He turned and followed, but, to his amazement, the moment she reached the road she turned back down the hill the way they had come. Clearly she could think of nothing but carrying the infant home to her father, and here even the slow perception of her companion understood her actions.

"Maggie, Maggie," he cried after her, "ye'll both be dead afore ye get home! Come on t' my mither. There never was a wuman like her for bairns! She'll ken better than any father what t' do wi't!"

Maggie at once recovered her senses, and knew he was right— but not before she had received an insight that was never afterward to leave her: now she understood the heart of the Son of Man, come to find and carry back the stray children to their Father and his. When afterward she told her father what she had then felt, he answered her with just the four words and no more.

"Lassie, ye hae it!"

Happily by now the moon had begun to inch its way up, so that Andrew was soon able to find the things they had dropped. Maggie wrapped the baby up in the winsey petticoat she had been carrying, for the night air was growing colder. Andrew picked up his loaf and other packages, and they set out again for Bogsheuch, Maggie's heart overwhelmed with gladness. She had not yet come to the point of asking what an infant could be doing alone on the moor; she was only exultant she had found it. Had the precious little thing been twice the weight, so exuberant were her feelings of wealth and delight that she could easily have carried it twice the distance, although the road was so rough that she was in constant terror of stumbling as she walked along.

Every now and then Andrew gave a little chuckle at the ludicrousness of their homecoming, and every so often had to stop and pick up one or another of his many parcels. But Maggie strode on in front, full of a sense of possession, and with the feeling of having at last entered into her heavenly inheritance. As a result she was almost startled when suddenly they came in sight of the turf cottage, in whose window a small oil lamp was burning. Before they even reached the door, Eppie appeared, welcoming them with an overflow of questions.

"What on earth—" she began.

" 'Tis a bonny wee bairnie, whose mither has left it!" interrupted Maggie, running up to her and laying the child in her arms.

Mrs. Cormack stood and stared—first at Maggie, then at the bundle that now lay in her own arms. Tenderly searching the petticoat, at last the old mother found the little one's face, and uncovered the sleeping child.

"Eh, the poor mither!" she said, and hurriedly recovered it.

"It's mine!" cried Maggie. "I found it honest!"

"It's mither may hae lost it honest, Maggie!" said Eppie.

"Weel, its mither can come for it, if she wants it. It's mine till she does anyway!" rejoined the girl.

"Nae doobt o' that!" replied the old woman, scarcely questioning that the infant had been left to perish by some worthless tramp. "Ye'll maybe hae it longer than ye'll care to keep it!"

"That's no very likely," answered Maggie with a smile as she stood in the doorway: "it's one o' the Lord's own lammies that he came to the hills to seek. He's found this one!"

"Weel, weel, my bonnie doo, it canna be for me to contradick ye!—But woe is me, for a foolish auld wife! Come in, come in, the more welcome that ye're so long expected!—But bless me, Andrew, what hae ye done wi' the cart, an' the beastie?"

In a few words, for brevity was easy to him, Andrew told the story of what had happened.

"It must hae been the Lord's mercy! The poor beastie has to suffer for the sake o' the bairnie!"

She got them their supper, which was keeping hot by the fire, and then sent Maggie to her bed in the *ben-end*, or inside the best room, where she laid the baby after washing him and wrapping him in a soft, well-worn shirt of her own. But Maggie could scarcely sleep, for listening to the baby's breathing lest it should stop. Eppie sat in the kitchen with Andrew until the light, slowly traveling round the north, deepened in the east and at last climbed the sky, leading up to the sun himself. Andrew then rose and set off toward Stonecross, which he reached before the house was yet astir, and then set about to feed and groom his horse.

All the next day Maggie was ill at ease, anticipating the appearance of the mother. The baby seemed nothing the worse for his exposure, and although thin and pale, appeared in other respects to be a healthy child, and took heartily the food offered him. He was decently though poorly clad, and very clean. The Cormacks made inquiry at every farmhouse and cottage within range of the moor, and the tale of the child's finding was quickly known throughout the entire neighborhood. But to Maggie's satisfaction nothing about the mother was discovered. By the time her visit came to an end, she was feeling tolerably secure in her new possession, and was anxious to return with it in triumph to her father.

The long-haired horse was not yet equal to the journey after its injury, and thus Maggie had to walk home. But Eppie accompanied her, bent on taking her share in the burden of the child, although it was with difficulty she persuaded Maggie to yield it even for a time. When they arrived and Maggie laid the child in her father's arms, the soutar rose from his stool and received him like Simeon taking the infant Jesus from the arms of his mother. For a moment he held him in silence, then restored him again to his daughter, sat down on his stool, and picked up his tool and a shoe. Then suddenly becoming aware of a breach in his manners, he rose again at once.

"I beg yer pardon, Mistress Cormack," he said. "I was clean forgettin' any breedin' I ever had!—Maggie, take oor frien' into the hoose, an' make her rest while ye get something for her after her long walk. I'll be in mysel' in a minute or two to hae a talk wi' her. I hae but a few mair stitches to put into this sole! The three o' us must take some serious coonsel t'gither aboot this God-sent bairn! I doobtna but he's come wi' a blessing to this hoose, but we must pray aboot what we're to do. An' we must pray for the mither o' him! Eh, but it was a merciful fittin' o' things t'gither that the poor bairn an' Maggie should that night come t'gither. The angels must hae been aboot the moor that day—even as they must hae been aboot the field an' the flock an' the shepherds an' the inn-stable on that gran' night!"

That same moment a neighbor entered, who had previously heard and misinterpreted the story, and now had caught sight of their arrival and had come to gather what gossip she could under the pretense of concern.

"Eh, soutar, but ye're a man sorely oppressed by Providence!" she said. "Who do ye think's been at fault there wi' yer daughter?"

The anger of the cobbler sprang up.

"Get oot o' my hoose ye ill-thinkin' woman!" he said, "an' comena here again except it be to beg my pardon an' that o' this good woman an' my bonny lass here! The Lord keep her frae ill-tongues!"

The outraged father, whom all the town knew for a man of the gentlest temper and great courtesy, stood towering. The woman stood one moment dazed and uncertain, then turned and fled. Maggie went into the house with Mrs. Cormack; and when the soutar joined them after completing his job, he never said a word about her. After Eppie had had some tea with them, she rose, bade them a good-day, and without visiting another house in the village, made her way back to her own cottage.

As soon as the baby was asleep, Maggie went back to the kitchen where her father still sat working.

"Ye're late tonight, Father," she said.

"I am that, lassie. But ye see I canna look for help frae you for some time noo. Ye'll hae enough to do wi' that bairn, an' we hae him to feed noo as well as oorsel's."

"It's little he'll want for a while at least, Father," answered Maggie. "But," she went on in a serious tone, "what kin' o' mither could leave her bairn oot there in the eerie night?—an' why?"

"She must hae been some poor lassie that hadna yet learned to think o' God's will first. Nae doobt she believed in some man, an' perhaps he promised to marry her, an' she didna ken he was a liar an' wasna strong enough to heed the voice inside her saying *ye mustna do it*. An' sae she let him do what he like wi' her, an' made himsel' the father o' a bairnie that wasna meant for him. She should never hae permitted such liberties to make a mither o' her afore she was merried. Such fools hae an' awful time o' it. For fowk is always lookin' doon on them. Doubtless, if it was like this, the rascal ran away and left her to fend for hersel'. An' naebody would help her, an' she had to beg bread for hersel' and a drop o' milk here an' there for the bairnie. Sae that at last she lost heart an' left it, jist as Hagar left hers beneath the bush in the wilderness afore God showed her the bonny well o' water."

"Do ye really think it happened sae, Father?" asked Maggie.

"Who kens, lassie? But 'tis not so unusual a story."

"I hardly ken which o' them was the worst—father or mither!"

"Nor do I!" said the soutar, "but if there were lies told, it must be the one that lied to the other who's counted the worse."

"There canna be many such men."

"'Deed there's a heap o' them," rejoined her father; "but woe for the poor lassie that believes them."

"She kenned what was right all the time, Father! She canna be blameless."

"That's true, my dautie. But to know is no aye to un'erstand. An' even to un'erstand is no aye to see right into a truth. No woman's safe—or man either—that hasna the love o' God, the great Love, in her heart all the time! What's best in her may turn to be her greatest danger. An' the higher ye rise ye come into the worst danger, till once ye're fairly in the one safe place, the heart o' the Father. There an' only there are ye safe—safe frae earth, frae hell, an' frae yer own heart! All the temptations, even such as made the heavenly hosts themselves fall frae heaven to hell, canna touch ye there! But when man or woman repents, an' humbles himsel', there he is to lift them up—an' higher than they ever stood afore!"

"Then they're no to be despised for their fall into sin?"

"None despises them, lassie but them that haena yet learned the danger they're in o' that same fall themsel's. Many a one, I'm thinkin', is kept frae fallin' jist because she's no far enough on to get the good o' the shame, but would jist sink farther an' farther."

"But Eppie tells me that most o' them that trips goes on fallin' an' never gets up again."

"Ow, ay—that's as true perhaps as far as we short-lived an' short-sighted creatures see o' them! But this world's but the beginnin', an' the glory o' Christ, who's the very Love o' the Father, spreads a heap further than that. It's not for naething we're told hoo the sinner women came to him frae all sides. They needed him badly, an' came. Never one o' them was too black to be let come up close to him, an' some o' such women un'erstood things he said that many respectable women couldna get a glimpse o'. There's aye rain enough in the sweet heavens, as Maister Shakespeare says, to wash the very hand o' murder white as snow. The creatin' heart is full o' such rain. Love him, lassie an' ye'll never dirty the bonny white gown ye brought frae his heart!"

The soutar's face was solemn and white, and traces of tears were running down the furrows of his cheeks. At length Maggie spoke.

"Supposin' the mither o' my bairnie is a woman like that, do ye think that *her* disgrace will stick to *him*?''

"Only in such minds as never saw the lovely greatness o' God.''

"But such bairns come na int' the world as God would hae them come!''

"But your bairnie *is* come, and that he couldna do withoot the creatin' will o' the Father! Doobtless such bairnies hae to suffer frae the prood judgment o' their fellow men an' women. But they may get much good an' little ill frae that—a good nobody can take frae them. Eh, the poor bairnie that has a father that would leave him an' his mither helpless. Such must someday be sore affronted wi' themsel's, that disgrace both the wife that should hae been, an' the bairn that shouldna. But he has another as weel—a right gran' lovin' Father to run to! The one thing, Maggie, that you an' me has to do, if the Lord sees fit for him to bide wi' us a spell, is never to let the bairn ken the missin' o' father or mither, an' sae lead him to the one Father, the only real an' true one.—There, he's wailin', the bonny wee man!''

Maggie ran to quiet the little one, but soon returned, and sitting down again beside her father, asked him for a piece of work.

And all this time, through his own indifference, the would-be-grand preacher knew nothing of the fact that somewhere in the world, without father or mother, lived and breathed a silent witness against him.

6 / The Vagrant _____

Isy managed to lengthen her visit to her grandmother, and thus postponed her return to her aunt's until James was gone, for she dreaded being in the house with him. She did return, however, and by and by the time came when she had to face the appalling fact that the dreaded moment was quickly approaching when she would no longer be able to conceal the change in her position.

Her first thought was how she could protect the good name of her lover from scandal, and avoid involving him in the coming ruin of her reputation. With this intent, she vowed, both to God and to herself, absolute silence concerning the past. Even James's name should never pass her lips!

And it was not that hard to keep the vow, even when her aunt took measures to draw her secret from her. Eventually her hour came, and she passed through it and found herself still alive, with her lips locked tight on her secret. In vain did her aunt ply her with questions, but she felt that to answer a single one of them would be to wrong him who had wronged her, and to lose her last righteous hold upon the man who had at least once loved her a little. He had most likely, she thought, all but forgotten her very existence by now, for he had never written to her, or made any effort to discover what had become of her. She clung to the conviction that he must never have heard that she had become pregnant.

At length she realized that to remain where she was would be the ruin of her aunt, for who would lodge in the same house with *her*! She must leave at once, yet she had not the least idea where she should go. Her exhausted physical condition, her longing to go, yet the impossibility of going at once, brought such despair to her mind, already weakened by the demands of the baby, that more than once she was on the point of taking poison. But the thought of her child gave her strength to live on. To add to her misery came the idea that—as fixed had been her resolve to silence—she had in some way been false to James, that she had betrayed him, brought him to shame, and forever ruined his prospects for advancement in the church. That must be why she never heard another word from him! She would never see him again!

All of these notions and convictions grew so steadily within her consciousness that one morning when her infant was not yet a month old, she crept out of the house and wandered out into the world, with just one shilling in the pocket of her dress.

Where she went and how she and the baby survived even she did not know. For a time her memory seemed to lose all hold upon her and everything about that time remained a blank. When she began to come to herself, it seemed that some weeks had passed, but she had no knowledge of where she had been or for how long her mind had been astray. Across the blank spaces of her brain were cloud-like trails of blotted dreams, and vague survivals of gratitude for bread and pieces of money. From what she could gather she had been heading north, first more-or-less along the eastern seaboard, then gradually inland. Everything she became aware of surprised her, except the child in her arms—already she could never forget him. Her sad story had been plain to everyone she met, and she had received thousands of kindnesses that her memory could not hold. At length, whether intentionally or not she did not know, she found herself on the road toward Banchory and Alford, and eventually in a neighborhood to which she had heard James Blatherwick refer.

Here again a blank came over her memory—till suddenly once more she came to herself and became conscious of being. She was alone on a wide moor in a dim night, with her hungry child. She had just given him the last drop of nourishment he could draw from her, and was now wailing in her arms. A great despair came over her, and unable to carry him another step farther, she laid him down from her helpless hands into a bush. He was starving and she must get him some milk! She went staggering about, looking under the great stones and into the clumps of heather for something he could drink, hardly knowing what she was doing. At last she sank onto the ground, herself weak from hunger, and fell into a kind of faint. When she came to herself, she searched all about for the child in vain, not even remembering the exact place where she had left him. This was the same evening when Maggie came along with Andrew and found the baby.

All that night, and a great part of the next day, Isy went searching all about the moor, but without finding the baby. Finally she discovered what she thought was the spot where she had left him, and not finding him there came to the conclusion that some wild beast had carried him off. A little ways off was a small peat-pond, and she immediately ran toward it with the thought of drowning herself. A man happened to be cutting peats nearby, saw her, threw down his spade and ran to stop her. He thought she was out of her mind, and tried to console her. He gave her a few halfpence and directed her to the next town. For a long time thereafter she wandered about, asking everyone she saw about the child, with alternating disappointment and expectation. Every day something happened that served to keep the life in her, and at last she reached the county-town, where she was taken to a place of shelter.

7 / The Preacher

James Blatherwick was proving himself not unacceptable to his native parish. He was thought to be a rising man, inasmuch as his fluency in the pulpit was far ahead of his insight. He soon came to take an interest in the soutar, noting him a man far in advance of the rest of his parishioners in certain spiritual matters, but at the same time he knew that he was regarded by many as a wild fanatic, if not a dangerous heretic. Because of this he perceived that for him to be accepted by the majority of his people, he would be on far safer ground to differ with the soutar rather than to agree with him, at least until his influence was more firmly established.

In Tiltowie he followed the same course as he had in the south, using the doctrinal phrases he had always been accustomed to, and that he knew his parishioners would be comfortable with. His chief goal was always toward eloquence. But not eloquence alone, but eloquence acknowledged as such by those who heard him. And this he had indeed largely already achieved—eloquence, that is, such as ignorant and wordy people value. But insight into truth as even his father and a few other plain people in the neighborhood possessed, he showed little sign of ever attaining.

He had noted that the soutar used almost none of the set religious phrases of the good people of the village, who devoutly followed the traditions of the elders. But he knew little as to what the cobbler did not believe, and still less of what he did believe. John MacLear could not even speak the name of God without a confession of faith immeasurably beyond anything inhabiting the consciousness of the parson. And on his part, the cobbler soon began to notice in young James a total absence of enthusiasm with regard to the things of the spiritual realm. Never did his face light up when he spoke of the Son of God, of his death, or of his resurrection. Never did he make mention of the kingdom of heaven as if it were anything more venerable than the kingdom of Great Britain and Ireland.

What exactly interested the young preacher in the old soutar it would be difficult to say. But the soutar's interest in James was a prayerful one; here was a young man, he could see, who needed more of the Son of Man than he presently had. Thus, toward that end he would be faithful to lift him up into the mind of his Father in heaven. Hence it was that the two began to have more and more to do with each other.

On one occasion the parson took upon himself to remonstrate with what seemed to him the audacity of his most unusual parishioner.

"Don't you think you are going just a little too far there, Mr. MacLear?" he said.

"Ye mean too far into the dark, Mr. Blatherwick?"

"Yes, that is what I mean. You speculate too boldly where there is no light to show what might be and what might not."

"But dinna ye think, sir, that that's the very direction where the dark grows a wee bit thinner, though I grant ye there's nothing yet to call light?"

"But the human soul is just as apt to deceive itself as the human eye. It is always ready to take a flash inside itself for something real," said Blatherwick.

"Nae doobt, nae doobt! But when the true light comes, ye aye ken the difference! A man *may* take the dark for light, but he canna take the light for darkness!"

"And there must always be something for the light to shine upon, otherwise the man sees nothing," said the parson.

"There's thought an' possible insight in the man!" said the soutar to himself. Then to Blatherwick, he replied, "Maybe, like the Ephesians, ye haena yet found oot aboot the Holy Spirit, sir?"

"No man dares deny that!"

"But a man might not *know* it, though he dares not deny it. None but them that follows where he leads can ken truthfully that he is."

"We must beware of private interpretation!" suggested James.

"If a man doesna hear the word spoken to his ain sel', he has nae word to trust in. The Scripture is to him but a sealed book; he walks in the dark. If a man has light, he has none the less that another's present. If there be two or three prayin' together, the fourth may hae none o' it, an' each one o' the three has jist what he's able to receive, an' what he kens in himsel' as light. Each one must hae the revelation into his ain sel'. An' if it be so, hoo are we to get any truth not yet revealed, 'cep' we go oot into the dark t' meet it? Ye must walk carefully, I admit, in the mirk, but ye must go ahead if ye would win at anythin'."

"But suppose you know enough to keep going, and do not care to venture into the dark and ask so many questions about things you don't know."

"If a man holds on practicin' what he does ken, the hunger'll wake in him after more. I'm thinkin' the angels desired long afore they could see into certain things they wanted t' ken aboot. But ye may be sure they werena left withoot as much light as would lead honest fowk safely on."

"But suppose they couldn't tell whether what they thought they saw was true light or not?"

"Then they would have to fall back upon the will o' the great Light. We ken well enough that he wants us all t' see as he himsel' sees. If we seek that Light, we'll reach it; if we carena for it, we're gaein' nowhere, an' may come in sore need o' some sharp discipline."

"I'm afraid I can't quite follow you. The fact is, I have been so long occupied with the Bible history, and the new discoveries that bear upon it, that I have had but little time for such spiritual metaphysics."

"An' what is the good o' history, or such metaphysics as ye call it as is the very soul o' history, but to help ye see Christ? An' what's the good o' Christ but sae to see God wi' yer heart an' yer un'erstandin' both as t' ken that ye're seein' him, an' sae to receive him into yer very nature? Ye mind hoo the Lord said that none could ken his Father but him to whom the Son would reveal him? Sir, 'tis time ye had a glimpse o' that! Ye ken naethin' till ye ken God—an' he's the only person a man truly can ken in his heart."

"Well, you must be a long way ahead of me, and for the present I'm afraid there's nothing for it but to say good-night to you."

And with the words the minister departed.

"Lord," said the soutar, as he sat guiding his awl through the sole and welt of the shoe he was working on, "there's surely somethin' at work in the yoong man! Surely he canna be that far from wakin' up to see and ken that he sees and kens nothin'. Lord, put down the dyke o' learnin' an' self-righteousness that he canna see over the top o', an' let him see thee on the other side o' it. Lord, send him the grace o' open eyes, to see where an' what he is, that he may cry oot wi' the rest o' us, poor blind bodies, to them that won't see, 'Wake, thou that sleepest, an' come oot o' thy grave, an' see the light o' thy grave, an' see the light o' the Father in the face o' the Son.' "

As the minister went away he was trying to classify the cobbler, whom he thought to place in some sect of the Middle-Age mystics. At the same time something strange seemed to hover about the man, refusing to be handled in that way. And from that day onward, the minister could not quite get the little man out of his mind. Something in his own heart, what he would have called his religious sense, could almost grasp a hint of what the soutar must mean, though he could neither isolate nor define it.

Faithless as he had behaved to Isy, James Blatherwick was not consciously—that is with purpose or intent—a deceitful man. On the contrary, he had always cherished a strong faith in his own honor. But faith in a thing, in an idea, in a notion, is no proof or sign that the thing actually exists. And in the present case it had no root except in the man's thought of himself. The man who thought so much of his honor was in truth a moral unreality, a cowardly fellow who, in the hope of escaping the consequences of his actions, carried himself as one beyond reproof.

The question must be asked how such a one would ever have the power of spiritual vision developed in him. How should such a one ever see God—ever exist in the same region as that in which the soutar had long lived? To be sure, such spiritual vision would never come without trials of some kind to open the doors of his heart. And James's had already begun, though he did not yet recognize them as such. But his hour was drawing closer.

Still there was this much reality in him, and he had made this much progress that, holding fast to his resolve never to slide again into sin, he was also aware of a dim suspicion of something he had not seen, but which he might become able to see. And a small part of him was half resolved to think and read with the intent to find out what this strange man seemed to know, or thought he knew.

8 / The Visit_____

James had of course seen Maggie on numerous occasions, whenever in fact he came to call on the soutar. Usually she sat silently
beside her father, both working away while the young parson con-
versed with the cobbler. However, he had not yet beheld the changes
readily evident in her since the days of their childhood. And neither
had he taken sufficient interest in the little household to ask who the
child was whom he had once or twice seen her ministering to with
such a tender show of devotion.

One day he went to call and knocked on the soutar's door. Maggie
opened it with the baby in her arms, with whom she had just been
having a game. Her face was in a glow, her hair tossed about, and
her dark eyes were flashing with excitement.

To Blatherwick, without any particularly great interest in life,
and in the net of a vaguely haunting trouble that was causing him no
immediate concern, the poor girl, below him in station, as he took
for granted, somehow struck him at the moment as beautiful. And
indeed she was far more beautiful than he was able to appreciate.
Besides, it had not been long since he had been refused by another,
and at such a time a man is all the readier to fall in love afresh. All
these factors had laid James's heart, such as it was, open to assault
from a new quarter from which he foresaw no danger.

"That's a very fine baby you have," he said. "Whose is he?"

"Mine, sir," answered Maggie with some triumph.

"Oh, indeed; I did not know," answered the parson, a little bewildered.

"At least," Maggie resumed a little hurriedly, "I have the best
right to him at the moment."

"She cannot possibly be his mother," thought the minister, and
resolved in his mind to question his housekeeper about the child when
he returned home.

"Is your father in the house?" he asked, but without waiting for an answer, went on, "but such a big child is too heavy for you to carry about."

"No one bit!" rejoined Maggie. "An' who's to carry him but me? Would ye hae my pet go travelin' the world upon his two bonny wee legs, wi'oot the wings he left ahind him? Na, na! they must grow a heap stronger first. His ain mamma would carry him if he were twice the size! Noo, come an' we'll go ben the hoose an' see Daddy."

They entered the kitchen, where Maggie sat down with the baby on her own stool beside her father, who looked up from his labor.

"Weel, Minister, hoo are ye today? Is the grave any lighter upon that top o' ye?" he said with a smile that looked almost cunning.

"I do not understand you, Mr. MacLear," answered James.

"Na, ye canna. If ye could, ye wouldna be sae comfortable as ye seem."

"I can't think why you should be rude to me, Mr. MacLear!"

"If ye saw the hoose on fire all aboot a man in a dead drunken sleep, maybe ye might not be in too great a hurry to be polite to him," remarked the soutar.

"Dare you suggest that I have been drinking?" cried the parson.

"Not for a single moment, sir. An' I beg yer pardon for causin' ye to think so. I don't believe ye were ever overtaken wi' drink in all yer life. An' perhaps I shouldna be sae ready to speak in parables, for it's not everybody that can or will un'erstand them. But ye canna hae forgotten that cry o' the Apostle o' the Gentiles—'Wake up, thou that sleepest!' For even the dead wake when the trumpet blast batters at their ears! What's impossible, ye ken, is possible, an' *very* possible, wi' God."

"It seems to me that the Apostle makes allusion in that passage to the condition of the Gentile nations. But may undoubtedly apply also to the conversion of any unbelieving man from the error of his ways."

"Weel," said the cobbler, turning half round, and looking the minister full in the face, "are *ye* converted, sir? Or are ye but turnin' frae side to side in yer coffin—seekin' a sleepin' assurance that ye're awake?"

"You are plain spoken anyway!" said the minister, rising.

"Maybe I am at last, sir. An' maybe I hae been too long comin' to the point o' bein' so plain. Perhaps I've been too afraid that ye would count me ill-fashioned—or what ye call rude."

The parson was already halfway to the door, for he was quite angry—which was hardly surprising. But with the latch still in his hand, he turned, and there was Maggie, standing in the middle of the floor with the child in her arms, looking as if she meant to follow him.

"Don't anger him, Father," said Maggie; "he disna ken better."

"Weel I ken that, my dautie. But I canna help thinkin' he's maybe no that far frae the wakin'. God grant I be right aboot that! Eh, if he would but wake up, what a man he would make! He knows a heap o' things—only what's that where a man has nae light!"

"I certainly do not see things as you would have me believe you see them," said Blatherwick, with the angry flush on his face intensified all the more at hearing the two speak thus about him. "And I fear you are hardly capable of persuading me that you do!"

The baby seemed to sense the anger in the room, for here it sent forth a potent cry. Clasping him close, Maggie ran from the room, jostling James in the doorway as he stood aside to let her pass.

"I am afraid I frightened the little man!" he said.

"'Deed, sir, it may have been you, or it may hae been me that frightened him," rejoined the soutar. "'Tis a thing I'm sore to blame in—that when I'm right in earnest, I'm aye too ready to speak almost as if I was angry. Sir, I humbly beg yer pardon."

"I too beg yours," said the parson. "I was in the wrong."

The heart of the old man was again drawn to the youth. He laid aside his shoe, turned on his stool, and said solemnly, "At this moment, sir, I would willingly die if by doin' so the light o' that uprisin' we spoke o' might break through upon ye."

"I believe you," said James, "but," he went on, with an attempt at humor, "it wouldn't be so much for you to do after all, seeing as how you would immediately find yourself in a better place!"

"Maybe where the penitent thief sat, some eighteen hunner years ago, waitin' t' be called up higher," rejoined the soutar with a watery smile.

The parson opened the door and went home—where his knees

found their way to the carpet, a place they had been none too familiar with till now.

From that day Blatherwick began to go more often to the soutar's, and before long went almost every other day, at least for a few minutes. And on such occasions generally had a short interview with Maggie and the baby as well, in both of whom, having heard the story of the child from the soutar, he took a growing interest.

"You seem to love him as if he were your own, Maggie!" he said one morning to the girl.

"An' isna he my ain? Didna God himsel' give me the bairn into my very arms—or all but?" she rejoined.

"Suppose he were to die," suggested the minister. "Such children often do."

"I needna think aboot that," she answered. "I would just hae t' say, as many a one has said afore me: 'The Lord gave'—ye ken the rest, sir."

Day by day Maggie grew more beautiful in the minister's eyes, until at last he was not only ready to say that he loved her, but to disregard any further worldy ambitions for her sake.

9 / The Proposal

On the morning of a certain Saturday—a day of the week he always made a holiday—Blatherwick resolved to let Maggie know without further delay that he loved her. His confession was made all the more imperative in that he was scheduled to preach for a brother clergyman at Deemouth in Aberdeen, and he felt that if he left his fate with Maggie unknown, his mind would not be cool enough for him to do well in the pulpit. But neither disappointment from a previous experience nor new love had yet served to free him from his vanity and arrogance: he regarded his approaching declaration as about to confer a great honor and favor upon the young woman of low background.

In his previous disappointment in the south he had asked a lady to descend a little from her social pedestal, in the belief that he offered her a greater than proportionate counter-elevation. And thus now, in his suit to Maggie where the situation was so greatly reversed, he was almost unable to conceive the possibility of her turning him down.

When he called, she would have shown him into the kitchen, but he took her by the arm, and leading her to the *ben-end* of the house, at once began his concocted speech. Scarcely had she gathered his meaning, however, when he was stopped by the startled look on her face.

"An' what would ye hae me do wi' the bairn?" she asked.

But the minister was sufficiently in love to disregard the unexpected interruption. His pride was indeed a little hurt that she should show more concern for a child than himself, but he resisted any show of it, reflecting that her maternal anxiety was not an altogether unnatural one.

"Oh, we shall easily find some experienced mother," he answered, "who will understand better than you how to take care of him."

71

"Na, na!" she rejoined. "I hae both a father an' a bairn t' look after. An' that's aboot as much as I'll ever be up to."

So saying, she rose and carried the little one up to the room her father now occupied, without casting a single glance of farewell in the direction of her would-be lover.

Blatherwick stood there astonished. Could it be that she had not understood his offer? It could hardly be that she did not appreciate his offer! Her devotion to the child was indeed absurdly engrossing, but that would be put right very soon. He need not fear such a rivalry as that, however unpleasant at the moment. The very idea of that little vagrant, from no one could tell where, coming between him and the girl he would make his wife—why the thing was preposterous!

He glanced around him. The room looked very empty! He heard her step above him through the thin floor; she was obviously walking back and forth with the senseless little animal. He caught up his hat, and with a flushed face of annoyance went straight out to the room where the soutar sat at his work.

"Mr. MacLear," he said, "I have come to ask you if you will give me your daughter to be my wife."

"Ow, so that's it!" returned the soutar without raising his eyes.

"You have no objection, I hope?" continued the minister, finding him silent.

"What does the lass say hersel'? Ye didna come to me first, I reckon."

"She said that she could not leave the child. But she cannot mean that."

"An' what for no? If that's her answer, then there's nae need for me to voice objections."

"But I shall soon persuade her to withdraw hers."

"Then I should have objections—more than one—to put t' the fore."

"You surprise me. Is not a woman to leave father and mother and cleave to her husband?"

"Ow, ay—if the woman is his wife. Then let none separate them! But there's anither sayin', sir, that may hae somethin' to do wi' Maggie's answer."

"And what is that?"

"That man or woman must leave father and mother, wife and child, for the sake o' the Son o' Man."

"You surely aren't papist enough to think that means a minister is not to marry?"

"Not at all, sir. But I hae nae doobt that's what it'll come to atween you an' Maggie."

"You mean that she will not marry?"

"I mean that she winna marry *you*, sir."

"But just think how much more she could do for Christ as a minister's wife."

"But what if she considered marryin' you as the same as refusing to leave all for the Son o' Man?"

"Why should she think that?"

"Because sae far as I see, she canna think that *ye* hae left all for him."

"Ah, so that is what you have been teaching her! She does not say that of herself! You have not left her free to choose!"

"The question never came up atween us. She's perfectly free t' take her ain way—an' she kens she is. Ye dinna seem to think it possible she should take *his* will rather than yours—that the love o' Christ should mean more to her than the love offered her by James Blatherwick."

"But allowing that you and I have different opinions on some points, must that be a reason why she and I should not love each other?"

"No reason whatever, sir—if ye can an' do. An' that may be a bigger *if* than ye realize. But beyond that, ye winna get Maggie to marry ye sae long as she disna believe ye love her Lord as weel as she loves him hersel'. It's no a common love that Maggie bears to her Lord, an' if ye loved her wi' a love worthy o' her, ye would see that."

"Then you will promise me not to interfere."

"I'll promise ye nothin', sir, excep' to do my duty by her—sae far as I un'erstand what that duty is. If I thought that Maggie didna love him as weel at least as I do, I would go upon my auld knees to her, an' entreat her to love him wi' all her heart an' soul an' stren'th an' mind. An' when I had done that, she might marry who she would—hangman or minister: no a word would I say. For trouble she must hae, an' trouble she will get—I thank my God, who giveth to all men liberally and upbraideth not."

"Then I am free to do my best to win her?"

"Ye are, sir, an' afore tomorrow I winna pass a word wi' her upon the subject."

"Thank you, sir," returned the minister, and took his leave.

"The makin's of a fine lad!" said the soutar aloud to himself as he resumed his work; "but his heart is no yet clear—no crystal clear—no clear like the Son o' Man."

He looked up and saw his daughter in the doorway.

"No a word, lassie," he said. "I'm unable t' talk wi' ye this minute. No a word to me aboot anythin' or anybody today, but what's absolute necessary."

"As ye wish, Father," rejoined Maggie. "I'm gaein oot t' see auld Eppie; I saw her in the baker's shop a minute ago—the bairnie's asleep."

"Very weel. If I hear him, I'll atten' t' him."

"Thank ye, Father," returned Maggie, and left the house.

Having to start that same afternoon for Deemouth, and still feeling it impossible to preach at his ease as long as things remained the way they were, the minister had hung about and was watching the soutar's door. When he saw it open and Maggie walk out, for a moment he flattered himself that she was sorry for her behavior to him and had come to look for him. But her start when she saw him satisfied him that such was not her intent. He quickly began to explain his presence.

"I've been waiting to see you, Margaret," he said. "I'm starting in an hour or so for Aberdeen, but I could not bear to go without telling you that your father has no objection to my saying to you what I please. He says he will not talk with you about me before tomorrow morning, and as I cannot possibly get back before Monday, I have no choice but to now express to you how real is my love. I admire your father, but he seems to hold the affections God has given us of small account compared with his judgment of the strength and reality of them."

"Did he no tell ye I was free to do or say what I liked?" rejoined Maggie rather sharply.

"Yes, he did say something to that effect."

"Then for mysel', I tell ye, Mister Blatherwick, I dinna care to see ye again, unless it be ye're callin' on my father, for I ken he's taken a great anxiety aboot ye."

"Do you mean what you say, Margaret?" said the minister, in a voice that betrayed not a little genuine emotion.

"I do mean it," she answered.

"Not even if I tell you that I am both ready and willing to take the child with you, and bring him up as if he was my own?"

"He wouldna *be* yer ain!"

"Quite as much as yours!"

"Hardly," she returned with a curious little laugh. "But I simply cannot believe ye love God wi' all yer heart. An' that is what matters most o' all in this."

"But dare you say that for yorself, Margaret?"

"No. But I do *want* to love God wi' my whole heart. An' God takes that almost as good as doin' it, leastways so my father always says. Mr. Blatherwick, are ye a real Christian? Or are ye sure ye're no a hypocrite? Ye have made it yer business to teach people man's chief end in life, which is to love God like that. But do ye yersel'? I would like t' ken. But I hae nae right t' question ye, for I dinna believe ye ken yersel'."

"Well, perhaps I do not. But I see there is no occasion to say more!"

"No, none," answered Maggie.

He lifted his hat and turned away to the coach office.

10 / The Realization_____

It would be difficult to represent the condition of mind in which James Blatherwick sat on the box-seat of the Defiance coach that evening behind four gray thoroughbreds, carrying him at the rate of ten miles an hour toward the coast. Hurt pride, indignation, and a certain mild revenge in contemplating Maggie's disappointment when at length she should become aware of the distinction he had gained and she had lost were its main components. He never noted a feature of the scenery that went hurrying past him, and yet the time did not seem to go slowly, for he was astonished when the coach stopped at Deemouth, and he found his journey at an end.

He got down rather cramped and stiff, and started out on a stroll about the streets to stretch his legs and see what was going on. He was glad he did not have to preach in the morning, and would have all afternoon to go over his sermon.

The streets were lit with gas, for Saturday was always a sort of market night, and at that moment they were crowded with girls going merrily home from the paper mill at the close of the week's labor. To his eyes, which had very little sympathy with gladness of any kind, the sight only called up by contrast the very different scene upon which his eyes would look down the next evening from the vantage point of the pulpit. The church would be filled with an eminently respectable congregation—to which he would be setting forth the results of certain recent geographical discoveries and local identifications, not knowing that already even later discoveries had rendered all he was about to say more than doubtful.

While sunk in a not very profound reverie, he was turning the corner of a narrow street when he was all but knocked down by a girl whom someone else in the crowd had pushed violently against him. Recoiling from the impact and unable to recover her balance, she fell on the granite pavement. Annoyed and half-angry, he began to walk on, paying no attention to the accident, when something in the pale face of the girl lying there motionless suddenly stopped him with the strong suggestion of someone he had once known. But almost the same instant the crowd gathered around and hid her from his view.

Shocked to find himself so unexpectedly reminded of Isy, he turned away and walked on, saying to himself that it couldn't possibly have been her. When he looked round again before crossing the street, the crowd had vanished, and the sidewalk was nearly empty. He spoke to a policeman who just then came up, but he had seen nothing of the occurrence, and remarked only that the girls at the paper mills were a rough lot.

In another moment his mind was busy with a passage in his sermon that seemed about to escape his memory. It was still impossible for him to talk freely and extemporaneously, and he memorized all his sermons. It was not out of the fullness of the heart that his mouth had yet spoken as a minister.

He went to the house of his friend Mr. Robertson whom he had come to assist, had supper with him and his wife, and retired early. In the morning he went to his friend's church, in the afternoon rehearsed his sermon, and when the evening came, climbed the pulpit-stair, and was soon engrossed in the rites of his delivery.

But as he seemed to be pouring out his soul in the long extempore prayer, he suddenly opened his eyes as if unconsciously compelled, and that same moment saw, in the front of the gallery before him, a face he could not doubt to be that of Isy.

Her gaze was fixed upon him; he saw her shiver, and knew that she saw and recognized him. He felt himself grow blind. His head swam, and he felt as if some material force was bending down his body.

Such was his self-possession, however, that he reclosed his eyes and went on with his prayer—if that could in any sense be called a prayer that he uttered without any feeling or true knowing behind the words themselves.

For the rest of the hour, through a mighty effort of the will, he maintained command of his thoughts and words and speech. He held his eyes fast that he might not see her again, but was constantly aware of the figure of Isy before him, with its gaze fixed motionless upon him. He began at last to wonder vaguely whether she might not be dead and had come back from the grave to haunt him as a mysterious thought-spectre.

But at the close of the sermon, when the people stood up to sing, she rose with them, and the half-dazed preacher sat down, exhausted with emotion, conflict, and effort at self-command. When he rose once more for the benediction, she was gone, and again he took refuge in the doubt whether she had indeed ever been present at all.

Later, after Mrs. Robertson had retired and James was sitting with his host over their tumbler of toddy, a knock came to the door. Mr. Robertson went to open it, and in a moment returned, saying it was a policeman to let him know that a woman was lying drunk at the bottom of his doorsteps, and to inquire what he wished done with her.

"I told him," said Mr. Robertson, "to take the poor creature to the station, and in the morning I would come and see if I could do anything for her. When they're ill the next day, sometimes you have half a chance with them; but it's seldom any use."

A horrible suspicion that it was Isy herself laid hold of James. For a moment he was almost inclined to follow the men to the station, but his friend would be sure to go with him, and then what might come of it! She had kept silent so long, however, it was probably that she had lost all care about him, and if left alone would no doubt say nothing. Thus he reasoned with himself against doing anything, lost in considerations of his own position and reputation, shrinking from the very thought of looking the disreputable creature in the eyes. Yet the awful consciousness haunted him that, if she had fallen into drunken habits and possibly worse, it was his fault, and the ruin of the once lovely creature lay at his door and his alone.

He went quickly to his room and to bed, where for a long while he lay, unable even to think.

Then all at once, with gathered force, the frightful reality, the keen bare truth broke upon him like a huge, cold wave. Suddenly he had a clear vision of his guilt, and the vision was conscious of itself as *his* guilt. He saw it rounded in a gray fog of life-chilling dismay.

What was he but a truth-breaker and a liar! "What am I," said his conscience, "but a cruel, self-seeking, contemptible sneak who, afraid of losing the praises of men, crept away unseen, and left the woman to bear alone our common sin?" What was he but a whited sepulchre, full of dead men's bones?—a fellow posing in the pulpit as an example to the faithful, but knowing all the time that somewhere in the land lived a woman—once a loving, trusting woman—who with a single word could hold him up to the world as a hypocrite?

He sprang to the floor; the cold hand of an invisible ghost seemed clutching at his throat. But what could he do? He felt utterly helpless, but in truth, though the realization of his guilt had at last dawned on him, he still did not dare look the question in the face as to what he could do. He crept ignominiously into his bed, and, gradually growing a little less uncomfortable, began to reason with himself that things were not so bad as they had seemed for a moment. He said to himself that many another had fallen in like fashion with him, but the fault was forgotten, and had never reappeared against him. No culprit was ever required to bear witness against himself! He must learn to discipline and repress his over-sensitivity, otherwise it would one day seize him at a disadvantage, and betray him into self-exposure.

Thus he reasoned, and he sank back into his former condition as one of the all but dead. The loud alarm of his rousing conscience ceased, and he fell asleep with the decision to get away from Deemouth the first thing in the morning before Mr. Robertson awoke and before anything about the girl should be done that might somehow involve him.

How much better it would have been for him to hold on to his repentant mood and awake to tell everything! But very few of his practical ideas, however much brooded over at night, lived to become live fruit in the morning; not once had he ever embodied in action an impulse toward atonement. He could welcome the thought of a final release from sin and suffering at the end of the world, but he always did his best to forget that at the very moment he was suffering because of wrong he had done for which he was taking not the least trouble to make the amends that were possible to him. He had lived for himself, to the destruction of one whom he had once loved, and to the denial of his Lord and Master!

More than twice on his way home in the early morning, he all but turned to go back to the police station. But it was, as usual, only *all but*, and he kept walking on to the coach-office.

11 / The Two Ministers

Even before James's flight was discovered in the morning, Mr. Robertson was on his way to do what he could for one of whom he knew nothing. The policemen returning from night duty found him already at the door of the office. He was at once admitted, for he was well known to most of them.

He found the poor woman miserably recovered from the effects of the night before. She looked so woeful that the heart of the good man immediately filled with profound pity. He recognized before him a creature whose hope was at its very end, to the verge of despair. She neither looked up nor spoke, but what he could see of her face appeared only ashamed, not sullen nor vengeful. When he spoke to her, she lifted her head a little, but not her eyes to his face. Tenderly, as if to the little one he had left behind in bed at his own house, he spoke to her child-soothing words of sympathy, which his tone carried to her heart, though she could hardly pay attention to the words. She lifted her lost eyes at length, saw his face, and burst into tears.

"Na, na," she cried, "ye canna help me, sir! There's naething that you or anybody can do for me! For God's sake, gie me a drink— a drink o' anything!"

"The thing to do you good is a cup of hot tea. You can't have had a thing to eat this morning. I have a cab waiting me at the door. Come home with me, my poor bairn. My wife'll have a cup of tea ready for you in a moment. You and me'll have our breakfast together."

"Ken ye what ye're sayin', sir? I darena look an honest woman in the face."

"I know a lot about folk of all kinds—more than you probably know yourself. I know more about you, too, than you think, for I've seen you in my own kirk more than once or twice. The Sunday night before last I was preaching straight into your bonny face, and saw you crying, and almost crying myself. Come away home with me,

83

my dear. My wife's another just like myself, and'll turn nothing to you but the smiling side of her face. She's a fine, hardy, good woman, my wife. Come and meet her!"

Isy rose to her feet.

"Eh, but I would like t' look once more into the face o' a bonny, clean woman!" she said. "I'll go, sir—only, I pray ye, sir, hurry an' take me oot o' the sight o' other folk."

"Ay, ay; we'll have you out of here in a moment," answered Mr. Robertson.—"Put the fine down to me," he whispered to the inspector as they passed him on their way out.

The man returned his nod and took no further notice.

"I thought that was what would come o' it," he murmured to himself, watching them leave with a smile. But indeed, he little knew what was going to come of it in the end!

The good minister, whose heart was the teacher of his head, and who was not ashamed either of himself or his companion, showed Isy into their little breakfast-parlor and then ran up the stair to his wife. He told her he had brought the young woman home, and wanted her to come down at once. Mrs. Robertson was in the middle of dressing their only child. She left the little one in the care of their one servant, and hurried downstairs to welcome the poor shivering bird of the night. She opened the door, stood silently for a brief moment, then opened her arms wide, and the girl fled to their shelter. But her strength failed her on the way, and she fell to the floor. Instantly the other was down by her side. Mr. Robertson hastened to her, and between them they got her on the couch.

"Shall I get the brandy?" said Mrs. Robertson.

"Try a cup of tea," he answered.

His wife hurried to the kitchen and soon had the tea poured out and cooling. But Isy still lay motionless. Then the minister's wife raised the helpless head on her arm, put a spoonful of the tea to her lips, and was delighted when the girl opened her mouth to swallow it. The next minute she opened her eyes, and would have risen, but the hand of the older woman held her down.

"I want t' tell ye," moaned Isy feebly, "that ye dinna ken who ye hae taken into yer hoose. Let me get up to get my breath, or I'll no be able t' tell ye."

"Drink the tea, and then say what you like. There's no hurry. You'll have time enough."

The poor girl opened her eyes wide and gazed for a moment at Mrs. Robertson. Then she took the cup and drank the tea. Her new friend went on: "You must just be content to bide where you are for a day or two. I have clothes enough to give you all the change you want."

"Eh, mem! Fowk'll speak ill o' ye if they see me in yer hoose!"

"Let them say what they please! What's folk but muckle geese!"

"But there's the minister, an' what people'll think o' him!"

"Hoots! What will he care?" said his wife. "Ask him yersell what he thinks of gossip!"

"Indeed," answered her husband, "I never heeded it enough to tell. There's but one word I heed, and that's my Master's."

"Eh, but ye canna lift me oot o' the pit!" groaned the poor girl.

"God helping, we can," returned the minister. "But you're not in the pit yet by a long road."

"I dinna ken what's to come o' me," she groaned.

"That we'll soon see! Breakfast's to come of you first, and then my wife and me will have a talk and see what's to be done. You can say what you please, and no ill folk will come near you."

A pitiful smile flashed across Isy's face, and with it returned the almost babyish look that used to form part of her charm. Like an obedient child she set herself to eat and drink what she could, and when she had evidently done her best, the minister took her cup and plate.

"Now, put your feet up on the sofa," said the minister, "and tell us everything."

"No," returned Isy. "I cannot tell you *everything*."

"Then tell us what you please—so long as it's true, and that I'm sure it will be," he replied.

"I will, sir," she answered.

For several minutes she was silent, as if thinking how to begin, then after a sigh or two, she spoke.

"I'm not a good woman," she began. "Perhaps I am worse than you think me.—Oh, my baby! my baby!" she cried, and burst into tears.

"We will not think badly of you," the minister's wife reassured. "But tell me just one thing: what made you go straight from the church to the public house last night? The two don't go so well together."

"It was this, ma'am," she replied, attempting to resume the more refined speech of the south "I had a dreadful shock that night from seeing someone in the church whom I had thought never to see again. And when I got out into the street, I turned so sick that somebody gave me a drink of whiskey, and, not having been used to it for some time, I disgraced myself. But indeed, I have a much worse trouble and shame upon me than that—one you would hardly believe, ma'am."

"I understand," said Mrs. Robertson, "and you saw him in church—the man that got you into trouble. I thought that must be it—won't you tell me all about it?"

"I will not name his name. I was the most to blame, for I knew better. And I would rather die than do him any more harm."

"Then don't say another word. I only thought it might be a relief to you. But I have no right to try to draw it out of you, and I wouldn't, except you want to tell me. I will never again ask you anything about him. There! you have my promise. Now, tell us what you please, and not a word more. The minister is sure to find something to comfort you."

"What can anybody say or do to comfort such as me, ma'am? I am lost—lost out of sight! Nothing can save me! The Savior himself wouldn't open the door to a woman that left her infant child out in the dark night! That's what I did!" she cried, and ended with a pitiful wail.

After a few moments she grew a little calmer, and then resumed.

"I would not have you think I wanted to get rid of the little darling. But my wits went all of a sudden, and a terror came upon me. Could it have been the hunger, do you think? I became frantic to find some milk for him, though what I was thinking of out on that barren moor I have not an idea. I laid him down in the heather, and ran from him. How far I went, I do not know. But whether I lost my way back, or what I did, or how it was, I cannot tell, only I could not find him. Then for a while I must have been clean out of my mind, and was haunted with visions of him being pulled at by the wild foxes. Even now, at night, every now and then it comes back, and I cannot get the sight out of my head. For a while it drove me to drink, but I got rid of that until just last night, when again I was overcome. Oh, if I could only keep from seeing them when I'm falling asleep!"

She gave a smothered scream and hid her face in her hands. Mrs. Robertson, weeping herself by now, tried to comfort her, but it seemed in vain.

"The worst of it is," Isy resumed, "—for I must confess everything, ma'am—is that I cannot tell what I may have done when the drink was on me. I may have even told his name, though I remember nothing about it. It must be months since I tasted a drop till last night. And now I've done it again, and I'm not fit for him even to cast a look at me. My heart's just like to break when I think I may have been false to him, as well as false to my bairn. If the devils would just come and take me I'd be grateful!"

"My dear," came the voice of the minister where he sat listening to every word she uttered, "nothing but the hand of the Son of Man will come near you out of the dark, soft-stroking your heart, and closing up the terrible gash in it. In the name of God, the Savior of men, I tell you, dautie, the day will come when you'll smile in the very face of the Lord himself at the thought of what he has brought you through—Lord Jesus, hold tightly to your poor bairn and to hers, and give her back her own. Thy will be done!—Go on with your tale, lassie."

" 'Deed, sir, I can say no more. I fear I'm still some sick."

She fell back on the sofa, her face very pale.

The minister was a big man. He took her in his arms and carried her to a room they always kept ready on the chance of a visit from "one of the least of these."

At the top of the stair stood their little daughter, a child of five or six.

"Who is it, mother?" she whispered as Mrs. Robertson passed, following her husband and Isy. "Is she very dead?"

"No, darling," answered her mother; "it is an angel that has lost her way, and is tired—so tired! You must be very quiet and not disturb her. Her head is going to ache very much."

The child turned and went down the stair, step by step, softly saying, "I will tell my rabbit not to make any noise—and to be as white as he can."

Once more they succeeded in bringing back the light of consciousness to Isy's clouded spirit. She woke in a soft white bed, with two faces of compassion bending over her, closed her eyes again with a smile of sweet contentment, and was soon wrapped in a wholesome slumber.

In the meantime the minister enslaved *to* himself rather than liberated *from* it as was his friend, had reached home and found a ghastly loneliness awaiting him at the manse. How much deeper it was even than that surrounding the woman he had forsaken! She had lost her repute and her baby; he had lost his God.

He had never seen the Almighty's shape, and did not have his Word abiding in him. And now the vision of him was closed in an unfathomable abyss of darkness. The signs of God were around him in the Book, around him in the work, around him in his fellow humanity, and around him in his own existence—but the external signs only! God himself did not speak to him, did not manifest himself to him.

God was not where James Blatherwick had ever sought him. He was not in any place where there was the least likelihood of his ever looking for or finding him.

12 / The Question

Blatherwick still knew nothing about the existence of his child. If he had, the knowledge might have altered the thoughts going through his mind on his way home to Tiltowie from the city, namely a half-conscious satisfaction he felt at having been preserved from marrying a woman who had now proved capable of disgracing him in the very streets. But at the same time he passed through many alternations of thought and feeling. Up and down, this way and that, went the changing currents of self-judgment or self-consolation, and of new dread of discovery. Never for two moments following one another was his mind clear, his purpose determined, his line set straight for honesty.

But in the end he sank again to that lowest of paths toward which his mind was ever bent: He must live up—not to the law of righteousness, but to the outward show of what a minister ought to be like. He must watch his appearance before men! He must keep up the deception he had begun in childhood, and had, until lately, practiced unknowingly.

Now that he knew what he was doing, he went on, not knowing how to get rid of it, shrinking in what must be regarded as cowardice from the confession that would have been the only thing able to set him free. Now he sought only how to conceal his deception. He was miserable in knowing himself to be not what he seemed—to be compelled to look like one that had not sinned. He grumbled in his heart that God should have forsaken him so far as to allow him to disgrace himself before his own conscience.

He did not yet see that his foulness, the sin that was part of his nature, was ingrained, that a man might change the color of his skin or a leopard his spots as soon as he would rid himself of that which was an intrinsic part of his being. He did not see that he had never yet looked purity in the face, that the fall which disgraced him in his own eyes was but the necessary outcome of his character—that it was no accident but an unavoidable result.

Even to begin the purification without which his moral and spiritual being must perish eternally, he would have to look on himself as he was. Yet he shrank from recognizing himself, and thought his true self lay hidden from all. It is strange to say, but many a man will never yield to see himself as he truly is until he becomes aware of the eyes of other men fixed upon him. Then first, ever to himself, will he be driven to confess what he has long all but known.

Blatherwick's hour was on its way, slow in coming, but no longer to be avoided. His soul was ripening to self-declaration. The ugly flower of self must blossom to show its nature for what it is. What a hold God has upon us in this inevitable ripening of the unseen into the invisible and present. The flower is there and must appear.

In the meantime he suffered, and walked on in silence, walking like a servant of the Ancient of Days, but knowing himself a whited sepulchre. Within him he felt the dead body that could not rest until it was laid bare to the sun; but all the time he comforted himself that he kept himself from falling a second time, and hoping that the *once* would not be remembered against him. Did not the fact that it was apparently forgotten, most likely never even known, indicate that he was forgiven of God? And so, unrepentant, he remained unforgiven, and continued a hypocrite and slave of sin.

But the hideous thing was not altogether concealed. Something was showing under the covering whiteness. His mother saw that something shapeless haunted him, and often asked herself what it could be, but always shrank even from conjecturing. His father, too, felt that he was removed a great distance from him, and that his son's supposed feeding of the flock had done nothing to bring him and his parents nearer to each other. What could be hidden, he wondered, beneath the mask of that unsmiling face?

But there was one humble observer who saw deeper than either of the parents—John MacLear, the village soutar.

One day, after about two weeks, the minister walked into the cobbler's workshop and found him there as usual. His hands were working away diligently, but his thoughts had for some time been brooding over the fact that God is not the God of the perfect only, but of the growing as well; not the God only of the righteous, but of such as hunger and thirst after righteousness.

"God, blow in the smoking flax, an' tie up the bruised reed!" he was saying to himself aloud when the minister walked in.

Now, as is the case in some other mystical natures, a certain something had been developed in the soutar very much like a spirit of prophecy. It took the form of an insight that occasionally laid bare to him in a measure the thoughts and intents of the heart of others, without the exercise of his will to that end. Perhaps it was rather merely the reasoning faculty of his mind working unconsciously, of putting together outward signs, and drawing from them the conclusion of the facts at which they pointed. In any case, he often found himself in the unusual position of seeing more deeply into another's heart than the other was aware of.

Upon this occasion, after their greeting, the soutar suddenly looked up at his visitor with a certain fixed expression. The first glance he had cast that day on the minister's face had shown him that he looked ill, and he now saw that something in the man's heart was eating away at it like a cancer.

Almost immediately the question arose in his brain: Could he be the father of the little one in the next room? But almost the same instant he shut it into the darkest closet of his mind, shrinking from the secret of another soul, as from lifting a corner of the veil that hid the Holy of Holies! The next moment, however, came the thought: What if it *was* true, and what if as a result the man stood in need of the offices of a true friend? It was one thing to pry into a man's secret; it was another to help him escape from it!

The soutar sat looking at him for a moment, as if out of this very thought, and as a result the minister felt the hot blood rush to his cheeks.

"Ye dinna look too weel, Minister," said the soutar. "Is there anythin' the matter wi' ye, sir?"

"Nothing worth mentioning," answered the parson. "I sometimes have a touch of headache in the early morning, especially when I have been up later than usual over my books the night before. But it always goes away during the day."

"Ow weel, that's no, as ye say, a very serious thing. I couldna help fanceyin' ye had somethin' out of the ordinary on your mind."

"Nothing, nothing," rejoined the minister, with a feeble laugh. "—But," he went on—and something seemed to send the words to his lips without giving him time to think—"it is curious you should say that, for I was just thinking what was the real intent of the Apostle in his injunction to confess our faults one to another."

The moment he had spoken the words he felt almost as if he had proclaimed his very secret from the housetop. He would have begun the sentence afresh, with some notion of correcting it, but again he felt the hot blood shoot to his face. *"I must go on with something!"* he thought to himself, *"or those sharp eyes of the old man's will see right through me!"*

"It came into my mind," he went on, "that I should like to know what *you* thought about the passage. It surely cannot give the least ground for directly spoken confession. I understand perfectly how a man may want to consult a friend in any difficulty—and that friend is naturally the minister, but—"

This was by no means a thing he had meant to say, but he seemed carried on to say he knew not what. It was as if the will of God was driving the man to the brink of a pure confession—to the cleansing of his bosom "of that perilous stuff that weighs upon the heart."

"Do you think, for instance," he continued, thus driven, "that a man is bound to tell *everything*—even to the friend he loves best?"

"I think," answered the soutar, making what effort he could to speak plainly so he would not be misunderstood, so important did he consider his words, "that we must answer the *what* before we enter upon the *how much*. An' I think, first o' all that we must ask, To *whom* are we bound to confess?—an' there surely is the answer, to him to whom we hae done the wrong. If we hae been grumbling in our hearts, it is to God we must confess: who else has to do wi' the matter? To *him* we must flee the moment oor eyes are opened to what we've been aboot. But if we hae wronged one o' oor fellow creatures, who are we to go to wi' oor confession but that same fellow creature? It seems to me we must go to that man first—even afore we go to God himsel'. Not one moment must we indulge procrastination on the plea o' prayin' instead o' confessin'. From oor very knees we must rise in haste, an' say to brother or sister, 'I've done ye this or that wrong: forgive me.' God can wait for yer prayer better than you, or him ye've wronged, can wait for yer confession! After that ye must make yer best attempt to make up for the wrong. 'Confess yer sins,' I think it means, 'each o' ye to the other against whom ye hae done the offense.'—Don't ye think that's the common sense o' the matter?''

"Indeed, I think you must be right," replied the minister, who was thinking of no such thing, but rather how he might recover his retreat. "I will go home at once and think it all over. Indeed, I am now all but convinced that what you say must be what the Apostle intended!"

With a great sigh of relief of which he was not aware, Blatherwick rose and walked from the kitchen, hoping he looked—not guilty, but sunk in thought. In truth he was unable to think. Oppressed and burdened down with the sense of a duty too unpleasant to even think about, he went home to his cheerless manse, where his housekeeper was the only person he had to speak to, a woman incapable of comforting anybody.

He went straight to his study, knelt down, but found he could not pray the simplest prayer. Not a word would come, and he could not pray without words. For the moment he was dead, and in hell—so far perished that he felt nothing.

He rose, sought the open air, but it brought him no restoration. He had not heeded his friend's advice. He was not even able to contemplate the thought of the one thing possible to him—had not moved even in spirit a step closer to Isy. The only comfort he could now find for his guilty soul was the thought that he could do nothing, for he did not even know where Isy was to be found. When he remembered the next moment that his friend Robertson must be able to find her—for if it was not her at his doorstep, she *did* at least occasionally attend his church. He soothed his conscience with the reflection that there was no coach till the next morning, and in the meantime he could write a letter. A letter would reach him almost as soon as he could himself.

But what would Robertson think? He might give the letter to his wife to read. They concealed nothing from each other. That would never do. So he only walked the faster, tired himself out, and earned an appetite as the result of his day's work. He ate a good dinner, although with little enjoyment, and fell asleep in his chair. No letter was written to Robertson that day. No letter of such sort was ever written. The spirit was not willing, and the flesh was weakness itself.

In the evening he took up a learned commentary on the Book of Job. But he never even approached the discovery of what Job wanted, received, and was satisfied with in the end. He never saw that what he himself needed, but did not desire, was the same thing—a sight of God! He never discovered that, when God came to Job, Job forgot all he had intended to say to him—did not ask him a single question—because he suddenly knew that all was well. The student of Scripture remained blind to the fact that the very presence of the Loving One, the Father of men, proved sufficient in itself to answer every question, to still every doubt. But then James's heart was not pure like Job's, and therefore he could never have seen God. He did not even desire to see him, and so could see nothing as it was. He read with the blindness of the devil of self in his heart.

In Marlowe's *Faust*, Mephistopheles says to the student:

> Where we are is hell;
> And where hell is there must we ever be:
> . . . .when all the world dissolves,
> And every creature shall be purified,
> All places shall be hell that are not heaven;

and it was thus that James fared; and thus he went to bed.

And while he lay there sleepless, his father and mother, some three miles away, were talking about him in bed.

13 / The Parents

Marion and Peter Blatherwick had lain silent for some time, thinking about their son. They had been reflecting how little satisfaction his being a minister had brought them. And in so thinking they had gone back in their minds to a certain time, long before, when they had had a talk together about him as a schoolboy.

Even then the heart of the mother had been aware of his coldness, his seeming unconsciousness of his parents as having any share in his life. Scotch parents are seldom outwardly affectionate to their children. But not the less in them, possibly all the hotter because of their outward coldness, burns the deep and central fire—that eternal fire without which the world would turn to a frozen mass, the love of parent for the child. That fire must burn while the Father of all men lives! That fire must burn until the universe *is* the Father and his children, and none beside. That fire, however long held down and crushed by the weight of unkindled fuel, must go on to gather heat, and, gathering, it must glow, and at last break forth in the scorching, yea, devouring flames of a righteous indignation: the Father must and *will* be supreme that his children perish not.

But as yet *the Father* endured and was silent, so too the child-parents must endure and be still. In the meantime their son remained hidden from them as by a thick moral hedge. He never came out from behind it, never stood clear before them, and they were unable to break through to him. There was no angelic traitor within his citadel of indifference to draw back the bolts of its iron gates and let them in. They had gone on hoping, and hoping in vain, for some change in him, but at last had to confess it a relief when he left the house and went to Edinburgh.

But the occasion of their talk about the lad was long before that.

The two children were in bed and asleep, and the parents were lying then, as they lay now, sleepless.

"Hoo's Jamie been gettin' on today?" said his father.

"Weel enough, I suppose," answered his mother, who did not then speak Scotch quite so broad as her husband's, although a good deal broader than her mother, the wife of a country doctor, would have permitted when she was a child. "He's always busy at his books. He's a diligent boy, but as to hoo he's gettin' on, I can't say. He never lets a word go from him as to what he's doin' one way or another. 'What *can* he be thinkin' aboot?' I sometimes say to mysel'—sometimes over and over. When I go into the parlor, where he always sits till he has done his lessons, he never lifts his head to show that he hears me, or cares who's there or who isn't. And as soon as he's done, he takes a book and goes up to his room, or oot aboot the house, or into the field or the barn, and never comes near me! I sometimes wonder if he would ever miss me dead!" she ended with a great sigh.

"Hoot awa, woman! dinna go on like that," returned her husband. "The laddie's like the rest o' laddies. They're jist like pup doggies till their eyes come open, an' they ken them that brought them here. He's bound to make a good man, an' he canna do that without learnin' to be a good son to her that bore him! Ye canna say he ever disobeyed ye. Ye hae told me that a hunner times!"

"I have that! But I would hae had no occasion to dwell upon the fact if he had ever given me, jist noo an' then, a wee sign o' any affection."

"Ay, doobtless, but signs are nae proofs. The affection o' the lad may be there, but the signs o' it missin'.—But I ken weel hoo the heart o' ye's workin', my ain auld dautie," he added, anxious to comfort her who was nearer to him than son or daughter.

He paused a moment, then resumed. "I dinna think it would be weel for me to say anything to him aboot his behavior to ye. It might only make things worse, for he wouldna ken what I was aimin' at. I dinna believe he has a notion of anythin' amiss in himsel', an' I fear he would only think I was hard upon him for nae reason. Ye see, if a thing doesna come o' itsel', no cryin' upon it will make it lift its head—sae long at least as a man himsel' kens naethin' aboot it."

"I'm sure ye're right, Peter," answered his wife. "I ken weel that scolding'll never make love spread oot its wings—except it be to flee away. Naethin' but fleein' can come o' scoldin'."

"It may do even worse than makin' him run," rejoined Peter. "Scoldin' may drive love clean oot o' sight. But we better go to oor ain sleep, lass!—We hae one anither, come what may."

"That's true, Peter. But aye the more I hae you, the more I want my Jamie!" cried the poor mother.

The father said no more. But after a while he rose, stole softly to his son's room. His wife heard him, and followed him, and found him on his knees by the bedside, his face buried in the blankets where his boy lay asleep with calm, dreamless countenance.

At length she took her husband's hand and led him back to bed.

"To think," she said as they went, "that he's the same bairnie I gazed at till my soul ran oot my eyes! I well remember hoo I laughed and cried both at once to think that I was the mother o' the manchild. An' I thought I then kenned what was in the heart o' Mary when she clasped the blessed one to her bosom!"

"May that same bairnie, born for oor remedy for sins, bring oor child to his right mind afore he's too auld to repent!" responded the father in a broken voice.

"Why was the heart o' a mither put into me?" groaned Marion. "Why was I made a woman, whose life is for the bearin' o' bairns to the great Father o' all, if this was to be my reward?—Na, na, Lord," she went on, interrupting and checking herself, "I want nothin' but thy will, an' weel I ken that ye wouldna hae me think such was thy will."

The memory of that earlier conversation took both the parents for a time into the silence of their own hearts. It would not be altogether truthful to say that they had taken no pleasure in the advancement of their son in the years since then. The mother was glad to be proud of his position, such as it was, in place of the happiness she could not find—proud with the love for him that lay incorruptible in her being. But the love that is all on one side, though it be stronger than death, can hardly be so strong as life! A poor, maimed, one-winged thing, such love cannot soar into any region of conscious bliss. Even when it soars into the region where God himself dwells, it is but to partake there of the divine sorrow that his heartless children cause him. But this poor pride notwithstanding, neither father nor mother dwelt much upon what their neighbors called James's success, or cared to talk about it. To do so they would have felt genuine hypocrisy so long as their relationship with him was so far from perfect. Never to anyone but each other did they allude to the bitterness of their own hearts. And now the daughter was also gone to whom the mother had at one time been able to unburden herself, because she understood and was able to share in her parents' misery over her brother.

So in silence the parents grieved, and the lad grew, and when James Blatherwick left Stonecross for the university, it was with scarce a backward look, with nothing in his heart but eagerness for the status that awaited him. He gained one of the highest bursaries, and never gave so much as a thought to the son of the poor widow who had competed with him, and who, because of his failure, had been forced to leave his ambition for an education behind him and go to work in a shop. This same young man, however, soon became able to keep his mother in what was to her nothing less than happy luxury, which is far more than can be said about the successful James.

As often as James returned home for the vacations, things between him and his parents were unchanged. By his third return, the heart of his sister had stopped beating any the faster at the thought of his arrival home: she knew that he would but shake hands limply, let hers drop, and a moment later be sat down to read. Before the time for him to take his degree came four years after he had begun, she had passed out of this life and to the great Father. James never missed her, and neither wished nor was asked to go home to her funeral. To his mother he was never anything more or less than quite civil, and on her part she never asked him to do anything for her. He came and went as he pleased, cared for nothing done on the farm or about the house, and seemed in his own thoughts and studies to have more than enough to occupy him. He had grown up to be a strong as well as a handsome youth, and had dropped almost every sign of his country breeding. He never spoke a word in his mother dialect, but spoke good English with a Scotch accent.

His father had to sadly realize that his son was far too fine a gentleman to show any interest in agriculture, or to put his hand to the least share in that oldest and most dignified of callings. His mother continued to look forward, although with fading interest, to the time when he should be the messenger of a gospel that he in no way understood. But his father did not at all share her anticipation.

He was an intelligent youth, and by the time he went to Edinburgh to learn theology he was relatively accomplished in mathematics, chemistry, and the classics. His first aspiration was to show himself a gentleman in the eyes of the bubblehead calling itself Society—of which in fact he knew nothing. After that his goal was to have his eloquence, at present existent only in his ambitious imagination, recognized by the public. These were the two devils, or rather the two forms of the one devil Vanity, that possessed him. He looked down on his parents, and on the whole circumstance of their ordered existence, as unworthy of him because it was old-fashioned and rural, concerned only with God's earth and God's animals, and having nothing to do with the shows of life. And yet to many the ways of life in the house of his parents, in contrast with the son's views of life, would have seemed altogether admirable. To such, the homely and simple ways of the unassuming homestead would have appeared very warm and attractive.

But James took little interest in any of this, and none at all in the ways of the humble people, tradesmen and craftsmen of the neighboring village. He never felt the common humanity that made him one with them. Had he turned his feelings into thoughts and words, he would have said, "I cannot help being the son of a farmer, but at least my mother's father was a doctor; and had I been consulted, my father should have been at least an officer in one of His Majesty's services, not a treader of dung or artificial manure!"

The root of his folly lay in his groundless self-esteem, fed by a certain literature that fed the notion that rising in the world and gaining the praise of men was the highest of callings. But the man whom we call *the Savior*, and who knew the secret of Life, warned his followers that they must not seek that sort of distinction if they would be the children of the Father who claimed them.

After both parents had lain silent for a good many moments, they began again to speak of their son.

"I was jist thinkin', Peter," said Marion, "o' the last time we spoke together aboot the laddie—it must be nigh six years since then, I'm thinkin'."

" 'Deed, I canna say. Ye may be right," replied her husband.

"It's no such a pleasant subject that we should hae much to say aboot it. He's a man noo, an' weel looked upon, but it makes little difference to his parents. He's jist as hard as ever, an' as far as man could weel be frae them he came frae—never a word to the one or the other o' us! If we were two dogs he couldna hae less to say to us. I'll bet Frostie says more in one half hoor to his tyke than Jamie has said to you or me since he first gaed away to college!"

"Bairns is a queer kind o' blessin'!" said the mother. "But, eh! it's what may lie behind the silence that frightens me!"

"What do ye mean, lass!"

"Ow, nothin' maybe," returned Marion, bursting into tears. "But all at once it was borne in upon me that there must be somethin' to account for the thing. At the same time I dare not ask God. For there's somethin' worse noo than was even there when he was a boy. He has such a look, as if he couldna see nor hear anythin' but what's inside him. It's an awful thing for a mither to say o' her own laddie, an' it makes my heart like to break!—as if I had feen false to my ain flesh an' blood!—Eh, Peter, what can it be?"

"Maybe it's nothin' at a'. Maybe he's in love."

"'Na, Peter. Love makes a man look up, not doon at his ain feet! It makes him hold his head back an' look oot in front o' him—no at his ain inside! It makes a man straight in the back, strong in the arm, an' bold in the heart. Didna it you, Peter?"

"Maybe it did; I dinna weel remember. But I see it can hardly be love wi' the lad. Still, even his parents mustna judge him, specially as he's one o' the Lord's ministers—maybe one o' the Lord's elect."

"It's awful to think—I hardly dare say it, Peter! But was no minister o' the gospel ever a heepocreete?—like one o' the auld scribes an' Pharisees? Oh, Peter, wouldna it be terrible if oor only ain son was—"

But here she broke down and could not finish the frightful sentence. The farmer left his bed and dropped into a chair beside it. The next moment he sank on his knees, and hiding his face in his hand, groaned, as from a thicket of torture.

"God in heaven, hae mercy upon the whole lot o' us!"

Then, apparently unconscious of what he did, he went wandering from the room, down the kitchen, and out to the barn on his bare feet, closing the door of the house behind him. In the barn he threw himself face downward on a heap of loose straw and lay there motionless. His wife wept alone in her bed, and hardly missed him. It required little reflection on her part to understand where he had gone or what he was doing. He was crying from the bitterness of a wounded father's heart, to the Father of fathers.

"God, ye're a father yerself'," he groaned, "an' sae ye ken hoo it's tearin' at my heart! I'm no accusin' Jamie, Lord, for ye ken weel hoo little I ken aboot him. He never opened the book o' his heart to *me*! Oh, God, grant that he has nothin' to hide; but if he has, Lord, pluck it oot o' him, an' *him* oot o' the mud! I dinna ken hoo to pray for him, Lord, for I'm in the dark. But deliver him some way, Lord, I pray thee, for his mither's sake!—Lord, deliver the heart o' her frae the awfulest o' all her fears—that her ain son's a hypocreet, a Judas-man!"

He remained there praying upon the straw while hour after hour passed, pleading with the great Father for his son; his soul now lost in dull fatigue, until at length the dawn looked in on the night-weary earth, and into the two sorrow-laden hearts, bringing with it a comfort they did not seek to understand.

14 / The Fire

But the prayers of his parents brought no solace to the mind of the weak, hard-hearted, and guilty son. He continued to succeed in temporarily soothing his conscience with some narcotic of false comfort, and even as his father prayed, he himself slept the sleep of the houseless, who look up to no watchful eye over them, and whose covering is narrower than they can wrap themselves in.

Ah, those nights! Alas for the sleepless human soul out in the eternal cold! But such was James's heartless state at present that if his mother had come to him in the morning with her tear-dimmed eyes, he would never have asked himself what could be troubling her, would not have had sympathy enough even to see that she was unhappy, would never have suspected himself as the cause of her red eyes and aching head. The only good thing in him was the uneasiness of his heart and the trouble of his mind, of which he was constantly aware.

Thank God, there was no way around the purifying fire! He could not escape it; he *must* pass through it!

15 / The Proposition_____

The world little knows what a power among men is he who simply and thoroughly believes in him who is Lord of the world to save men from their sins! He may be neither wise nor prudent in the world's eyes. He may be clothed in no attractive colors or in any word of power. And yet if he has but that love for his neighbor that is rooted in and springs from love to his God, he is always a redeeming, reconciling influence among his fellows. The Robertsons were genial of heart, loving and tender toward man or woman in need of them, and their door was always open for such to enter and find help. If the parson insisted on the wrath of God against sin, he did not fail to give assurance of the Lord's tenderness toward such that had fallen.

Together the godly pair at length persuaded Isobel of the eager forgiveness of the Son of Man. They assured her that he could not drive from him the very worst of sinners, but loved—nothing less than tenderly loved—anyone who turned his face to the Father. She would no doubt, they said, have to bear her trespass in the eyes of the unforgiving who looked upon her, but the Lord would lift her high and welcome her to the home of the glad-hearted.

But poor Isy, who regarded her fault as both against God and the man who had misled her, was sick at heart. She insisted that nothing God himself could do could ever restore her, for nothing could erase the fact that she had fallen. God might be ready to forgive her, but could not love her! Jesus might have made satisfaction for her sin, but how could that make any difference in or to her? She was troubled that Jesus should have so suffered, but that could not give her back her purity, or the peace of mind she once possessed. That was gone forever! Never to all eternity could she be innocent again. Life had lost all interest for her.

And yet, strange to say, along with this suffering of mind came a requickening of her long dormant imagination. Sometimes she would wake from a dream where she stood in blessed nakedness with

105

a deluge of cool, comforting rain pouring upon her from the sweetness of heaven. And every night to her sinful bosom came back the soft innocent hands of the child she had lost. But then she would always dream that she was Hagar, casting her child away, and fleeing from the sight of his death. More than once she dreamed that an angel came to her, and went out to look for her boy—only to return and lay him in her arms, dead from some wild beast.

When the first few days of her sojourn with the good Samaritans were over, and she had gathered enough strength to feel she ought not to burden them any longer, they positively refused to let her leave. They began to try to revive her spirits by reawakening in her the hope of finding her lost child. They set inquiry on foot in every direction, and promised to let her know the moment they began to feel inconvenienced by her presence.

"Inasmuch as ye did it to one of the least of these, ye did it to me!" insisted Mrs. Robertson upon one of the poor girl's outbursts of self-pity. "Was the Lord a burden to Mary and Lazarus?"

"But that doesn't apply to me, ma'am," objected Isy. "I'm none of his!"

"Who is then? Whom did he come to save? Are you not one of his lost sheep? Are you not weary and heavy-laden? Will you never let him feel at home with you? Are *you* to say who he is to love and who he isn't? Are *you* to tell him who are fit to be counted his, and who are not good enough?" Isy was silent for a long time. The foundations of her coming peace were being dug deeper and laid wider.

Isy still found it impossible, from the disordered state of her mind, to give any careful thought to where she had laid her child down. And Maggie, who loved him passionately, and believed him willfully abandoned, had no desire to discover one who could claim him, but was unworthy of him. Therefore, for a long time neither she nor her father ever talked, or encouraged talk about him. Nevertheless, certain questioning busybodies began to sniff about and give tongue. It was all very well, they said, for the cobbler and his Maggie to pose as rescuers and benefactors; but whose was the child? His growth nevertheless went on all the same, and however such hints might seem to concern him, happily they never reached him. And yet all the time, in the not so distant city, a loving woman was weeping and pining for lack of him, whose conduct, in the eyes of the Robertsons, was blameless. But although mentally and spiritually she was growing rapidly, she seemed to have lost all hope. For deeper in her soul, and nearer the root of her misery than even the loss of her child, lay the character and conduct of the man whom she had loved. His neglect of her burned at the bands of her life; and her friends soon began to fear that she was on the verge of a slow downward slide upon which there is seldom any turning.

Mr. and Mrs. Robertson had long been on very friendly terms with the farmer of Stonecross and his wife. And thinking about the condition of their guest, it was natural that the thought of Mrs. Blatherwick should occur to them as one who might be able to give the kind of help the poor girl needed. Since the death of their own daughter, they had not even had a servant with them at the farm, and the parson thought that the potential relationship could not help but be beneficial to both sides. He decided, therefore, to pay their friends at Stonecross a visit and tell them all they knew about Isy.

It was a lovely morning in the decline of summer when the minister mounted the top of the coach, to wait, silent and a little anxious, for the appearance of the coachman from the office, after which he thrust the waybill into the pocket of his huge greatcoat, to gather his reins and climb heavily to his perch. A journey of four hours, through a not very interesting country, but along a splendid road in the direction of Inverness, would carry him to the village where the soutar lived and where James Blatherwick was parson. Passing through gentle rolling farmland, the corn was nearly full grown, but still green, without sign of the coming gold of perfection that was still some weeks away. After his arrival in Tiltowie, a walk of about three miles awaited him—a long and somewhat weary way to the town-minister—accustomed indeed to tramping the hard pavements, but not to long walks unbroken by calls.

Climbing at last the hill on which the farmhouse stood, he caught sight of Peter Blatherwick in a nearby field of barley stubble, with the reins of a pair of powerful Clydesdales in his hands, wrestling with the earth as it strove to wrench from his hold the stilts of the plough whose share and coulter he was guiding through it. Peter's delight was in the open air, and hard work in it. He was far above the vulgar idea that a man rises in the social scale to the degree he ceases to labor with his hands. No more could he have imagined that a man advances in the kingdom of heaven by being made an elder.

As to his higher nature, the farmer believed in God—that is, he tried to do what God required of him, and thus was on the straight road to know him. He talked little about religion, and was not one to take sides on doctrinal issues. When he heard people advocating or opposing the claims of this or that party in the church, he would turn away with a smile such as men yield to the talk of children. He had no time, he would say, for that kind of thing. He had enough to do in trying to faithfully practice what was beyond dispute.

He was a reading man, one who not merely drank at every open source he came across, but thought over what he read, and was therefore a man of true intelligence, who was regarded by his neighbors with more than ordinary respect. He had been the first in the district to apply certain discoveries in chemistry to agriculture, and had made use of them with notable results on his own farm, and setting an example which his neighbors were so ready to follow that the region, nowise remarkable for its soil, soon became rather remarkably known for its crops.

The noteworthiest thing in him, however, was his *humanity*, shown first and chiefly in the width and strength of his family affections. He had a strong drawing, not only to his immediate relations, but to all of his blood, and they were many, for he came of an old family that had been long settled in the neighborhood. In worldly affairs, he was better than most of the region, having added not a little to the small amount of land his father had left him. But he was by no means a lover of money, being open-handed to his wife, upon whom a miser is usually the first to exercise his parsimony. There was, however, at Stonecross, little call for the spending of money, and still less temptation from without, for the simple life of the Blath-erwicks was supplied in most of its necessities from the farm itself. In disposition Peter was a good-humored, even merry, man, with a playful answer almost always ready for a greeting neighbor.

The minister waved a greeting to the farmer from a distance and went first to the house, which stood close at hand, with its low gable toward him.

Mr. Robertson passed a low window, through which he had a glimpse of the pretty old-fashioned parlor within, as he went round to the front to knock at the nearer of two green-painted doors.

Mrs. Blatherwick came to open it, and finding who it was that knocked—of all the men the most welcome in her present mood of disconsolation over her son—received him with the hearty simplicity of an evident welcome. Though she was not yet prepared to open her heart and let him see into its sorrow, the appearance of the minister brought her, nevertheless, as it were the dawn of a winter morning after a long night of pain.

She led him into the low-ceiled parlor and into the green gloom of the big hydrangea that filled the front window, and the ancient scent of the withered rose-leaves in the gorgeous china on the gold-bordered table-cover. There the minister sat, and after a few commonplaces silently pondered how to make the proposition he had in his mind.

Marion Blatherwick was a good-looking woman, with a quiet strong expression, and sweet gray eyes. The daughter of a country surgeon, she had been left an orphan without means, but was so generally respected that everyone said Mr. Blatherwick had never done better than when he married her. There had very early grown up a sense of distance between her and her son, and now her heart would sometimes go longing after him as if he were one of those who died in their infancy. But her dead daughter, gone beyond range of eye and ear, seemed never to have left them: there was no separation, only distance between them.

"I have taken the liberty, Mrs. Blatherwick, of coming to ask your help in a great perplexity," began Mr. Robertson, with a hesitancy she had never seen in him before.

"Weel, sir, 'tis an honor to me, I'm sure!" she answered.

"Wait until you hear what it is," rejoined the minister. "We, that is, my wife and I, have a poor lass at home with us. We've taken a great interest in her for some weeks past, but now we're almost at our wits' end about what to do with her next. She's sad in heart and not in the best of health and altogether without hope. And she stands in a desperate need of a change.''

"Weel, that ouchtna be much o' a difficulty atween auld frien's like oorsel's. Mr. Robertson! Ye would hae us take her in for a while, till she begins to look up a bit, poor thing? Hoo auld is she?''

"She can hardly be more than twenty, or about that—near what your own lassie would have been by this time, if she had ripened here instead of going away to the grand finishing school of the just made perfect. And, indeed, she's not altogether unlike your own lass.''

"Eh, sir, bring her to me! My heart's waitin' for her. But what aboot her ain mither? She maunna lose her!''

"She has no mother! But I don't want you to do anything hastily. I must tell you about her first.''

"I'm content that she's a friend o' yers. I weel ken ye would never hae me take into my hoose one what wasna fit.''

"The fact is, she's had a terrible misfortune.''

The good woman drew back slightly, then asked hurriedly.

"There's no bairn, is there?''

"Indeed there is—but part of the misery is that the child's disappeared, and she's breaking her heart over him. She's almost out of her mind, ma'am! Not that she's anything but perfectly reasonable, and she never gives us a grain of trouble. And I can't doubt but that she'd be a great help to you for however long you would let her stay. But she's just haunted with the idea that she put the baby down and left him, and she doesn't know where. Truly ma'am, I think she's one of the lambs of the Lord's own flock!''

"That's no the way the lambs o' *his* flock are in the way o' behavin' themsel's! I fear, sir, that ye may be lettin' yer heart run away wi' yer judgment.''

"I have always considered Mary Magdalene one of the Lord's own lambs, that he left the rest to look for, and this is such another. If you help him to come upon her, you'll carry her home between you rejoicing. And you'll remember how he stood between one far worse than her and the men that fain would have shamed her, and then he sent them away like so many dogs—those great Pharisees—with their tails between their legs.''

"Ay, ye're right, sir!" cried his hostess. "To think that my heart should hae made me doobt yer word as one o' the Lord's servants, I beg yer pardon. Will ye no bide the night wi' us an' go back by the mornin' coach?"

"I will that, ma'am—and I thank you kindly! I am a bit fatigued with the hill road, and the walk was a bit longer than I'm used to."

"Then I must go an' see aboot dinner," said Marion, rising. "I winna be long."

Later, after the farmer had anticipated the hour for unyoking and had hurried home, they enjoyed their dinner together, and then sat in the cool of a sweet summer evening in the garden in front of the house, among roses and lilies and poppy heads and long pink-striped grasses. The minister opened wide his heart and told them all he knew and thought about Isy. And so prejudiced were they in her favor by what he said of her that whatever anxieties might have yet remained about the new relation into which they were about to enter were soon absorbed in the hopeful expectation of her appearance. Indeed, the prospect of aiding one in the effort to rise to a new life was the best comfort he could have brought them in their own miseries about James.

When he reached home, the minister was startled, even dismayed by the pallor that came over Isy's face when she heard the name and abode of the friends that he assured her would welcome her warmly.

"They'll be wanting to know everything!" she sobbed.

"You tell them everything they have a right to know," returned the minister. "They are good people, and will not ask more. Beyond that, they will respect your silence."

"There's one thing, as you know, that I can't and won't tell. To hold my tongue about that is the one particle of honesty left possible to me. It's enough that I should have been the cause of the poor man's sin, and I'm not going to bring upon him any of the consequences of it as well."

"We will not go into the question of whether you or he was the more to blame," returned the parson, "but I heartily approve of your resolve, and admire your firmness in holding to it. The time *may* come when you *ought* to tell; but until then, I shall not even allow myself to wonder who the faithless man may be."

Isy burst into tears.

"Don't call him that, sir! Don't drive me to doubt him. I deserve nothing! And for my bonny bairn, he must by this time be back home to Him that sent him!"

Thus assured that her secret would be respected by those to whom she was going, Isy ceased to show further reluctance to accept the shelter offered her. And in truth, underneath the dread of encountering James Blatherwick's parents, lay hidden in her mind the fearful joy of catching a chance glimpse of the man whom she still loved with the forgiving tenderness of a true, therefore a strong heart.

With a trembling, fluttering bosom therefore, she took her place not many days thereafter on the coach beside Mr. Robertson, to go with him to the refuge he had found for her.

16 / The Refuge

Once more out in the country, the beauties of the world began to work the will of its Maker upon Isy's poor lacerated soul. And afar in its hidden deeps the process of healing was already begun. Sorrow would often return unbidden, would at times even rise like a crested wave and threaten despair, but the Real and the True, long hidden from her by false treatment and by the lying judgments of men and women, was now at length beginning to reveal itself to her tear-blinded vision. Hope was lifting a feeble head above the tangled weeds of the subsiding deluge, and before long the girl would be able to see and understand how little the Father, whose judgment in the truth of things, cares what at any time his child may have been or done the moment that child gives herself up to be made what he would have her! Looking down into the hearts of men, he sees differences there of which the self-important world takes no heed. For indeed, many that count themselves of the first, he sees the last—and what he sees, alone *is*. Kings and emperors may be utterly forgotten, while a gutter-child, a thief, a girl who in this world never had even a notion of purity, may lie smiling in the arms of the Eternal, while the head of a lordly house that still flourishes like a green bay-tree, may be wandering about with the dogs beyond the walls of the city.

In the open world, the power of the present God began at once to influence Isobel, for there, although dimly, she yet looked into his open face, sketched vaguely in the mighty something we call nature—chiefly on the great vault we call heaven. Shapely but undefined; perfect in form, yet limitless in depth; blue and persistent, yet ever evading capture by human heart in human eye; this sphere of fashioned boundlessness, of definite shapelessness, called up in her heart the formless children of upheavedness—grandeur, namely, and awe, hope and desire: all rushed together toward the dawn of the unspeakable One, who, dwelling in that heaven, is above all heavens; mighty and unchangeable, yet childlike; inexorable, yet tender as never was mother; devoted as never yet was any child except one. Isy, indeed, understood little of all this; yet she wept, she knew not why; and it was not for sorrow.

When the coach journey was over, and she turned her back upon the house where her child lay and entered the desolate hill-country, a strange feeling began to invade her counsciousness. It seemed at first but an old mood, worn shadowy; then it seemed like the return of an old dream, then a painful, confused, half-forgotten memory. But at length it cleared and settled into a conviction that she had been in the same region before, and had had, although a passing, yet a painful acquaintance with it. And finally she concluded that she must be near the spot where she had left and lost her baby.

Suddenly everything that had befallen her became fused in her mind into a troubled conglomerate of hunger and cold and weariness, of help and hurt, of deliverance and returning pain. They all mingled with the scene around her, and there condensed into the memory of that one event—of which this must assuredly be the actual place! She looked upon the widespread wastes of heather and peat, great stones here and there, half buried in it, half sticking out of it. Surely she was waiting there for something to come to pass! Surely behind this veil of the seen, a child must be standing with outstretched arms, hungering after his mother!

But just as suddenly, alas!, her certainty of recollection faded from her, and of the memory itself remained nothing but a ruin. And all the time it took to dawn into brilliance and fade back out into darkness had measured but a few weary steps by the side of her companion, who was himself lost in the glad meditation of a glad sermon for the next Sunday about the lost sheep carried home with jubilance, forgetting all the while how unfit was the poor sheep beside him for such a fatiguing tramp up hill and down, along what was little more than the stony bed of a winter's torrent of a stream.

All at once Isy darted aside from the rough track, scrambled up the steep ban, and ran like one demented into a great clump of heather, through which she began to search with frantic hands. The minister stopped bewildered and stood to watch her, almost fearing for a moment that she had again lost her wits. She got on top of a stone in the middle of the slump, turned several times around, gazed in every direction over the moor, then descended with a hopeless look, and came slowly back to him.

"I beg your pardon," she said. "I thought I had a glimpse of my infant through the heather. I am sure this is the very spot where I left him!"

Then the next moment she faltered and said, "Have we far to go yet, sir?" and before he could even give her an answer, she staggered to the bank at the side of the road and fell upon it.

The minister saw at once that he had been pushing her too hard. He stooped down and tried to help her to lie comfortably on the short grass, and then waited anxiously for her to recover. He could see no water nearby, but at least she had plenty of air!

In a little while she came to herself, sat up, and would have risen to resume the journey except that the minister, filled with compassion for her, picked her up in his arms and carried her to the top of the hill. She argued, but was unable to resist. Light as she was, however, he found it no easy task to bear her up the last part of the steep rise, and was glad to set her down at the top—where a fresh breeze was waiting to revive them both. She thanked him like a child whose father had come to her help, and they seated themselves together on the highest point of the moor, with a large, desolate stretch of land on every side of them.

"Oh, but you *are* good to me!" she said. "That just reminded me of the Hill of Difficulty in the *Pilgrim's Progress*!"

"Oh, you know the story?" said the minister.

"My old grannie used to make me read it to her when she lay dying. I thought it long and tiresome then, but since you took me to your house, sir, I have remembered many things in it. I knew then that I was come to the house of the Interpreter. You've made me understand."

"I am glad of that, Isy! You see, I know some things that make me very glad, and so I want them to make you glad too. And the thing that makes me gladdest of all is just that God is what he is. To know that such a one is God over us and in us makes our very being a most precious delight. His children, those of them that know him, are all glad just because he *is* and they are his children. Do you think a strong man like me would read sermons and say prayers and talk to people, doing nothing but shamefully easy work if he did not believe what he said?"

"I'm sure you have had hard enough work with me! I am a hard one to teach. I was in such a bog of ignorance and misery, but I think I am now getting my head up out of it. But please, let me ask you one thing: How is it that when the thought of God comes to me, I draw back as if I were afraid of him? If he be the kind of person you say he is, why can't I go close up to him?"

"I confess the same foolishness, my child, at times," answered the minister. "It can only be because we do not yet see God as he is—and that must be because we do not yet really understand Jesus— do not see the glory of God in his face. God is just like Jesus— exactly like him!"

The parson fell to wondering, as he had many times in the past, how it could be that so many, gentle and guiltless as this woman-child, recoiled from the thought of the perfect One. Why should they not be always and irresistibly drawn toward the very idea of God, instead of afraid of him? Why, at least, should they not run to see and make sure whether God was indeed such a one or not? whether he was really Love itself?

They sat thinking and talking, with silences between. And while they thought and talked, the daystar was all the time rising unnoticed in their hearts. At length, finding herself much stronger, Isy rose, and they resumed their journey.

The door of the farmhouse stood open to receive them. But even before they reached it, a bright-looking little woman, with delicate lines of ingrained red in a sorrowful face, appeared in it, looking out with questioning eyes—like a mother bird just loosening her feet from the threshold of her nest to fly and meet them. Through the film that blinded those expectant eyes, Marion saw what manner of woman she was that drew nigh, and her motherhood went out to her. For in the love of Isy's yearning look, humbly seeking acceptance, and in her hesitating approach half-checked by gentle apology, Marion imagined she saw her own daughter coming back from the gates of death and sprang to meet her.

The meditating love of the minister obliterated itself, making him linger a step or two behind, waiting to see what would follow. When he saw the two folded each in the other's arms, and the fountain of love thus break forth from their encountering hearts, his soul leaped for joy of the new-created love—new, but not the less surely eternal. For God is love, and love is that which is, and was, and shall be for evermore—boundless, unconditional, self-existent, creative! "Truly," he said to himself, "God is love, and God is all in all! In him love evermore breaks forth anew into fresh personality—in every new consciousness, in every new child of the one creating Father. In every burning heart, in everything that hopes and fears and is, love is the creative presence, the center, the source of life, yea, life itself; yea, God himself!"

The elder woman drew herself a little back, held the poor white-faced thing at arms' length, and looked her through the face into the heart.

"My bonny lamb," she said, and hugged her close, "come home and be a good bairn, and no ill man shall touch ye again. There's *my* man waitin' for ye, to keep ye safe!"

Isy looked up, and over the shoulder of her hostess saw the strong paternal face of the farmer, full of silent welcome. He did not try to account for the strange emotion that filled him.

"Come in, lassie," he said, and led the way through the parlor, where the red sunset was shining through the low gable window, filling the place with the glamour of departing glory. "Sit ye doon on the sofa there; ye must be tired. Surely ye haena come all the long road frae Tiltowie upon yer ain two wee feet?"

"'Deed she has," answered the minister, who had followed them into the room.

Marion lingered outside, wiping away the tears that insisted on continuing to flow. For the one question, "What can be amiss wi' Jamie?" had returned upon her, haunting her heart. And with it had come the idea, though vague and formless, that their goodwill to the wandering outcast might perhaps do something to make up for whatever ill thing their James might have done. At last, instead of entering the parlor, she turned away into the kitchen to make their supper.

Isy sank back in the wide sofa, lost in refuge, and when he saw the look on her face, the minister said to himself, "She is feeling just as we shall all feel when first we know that nothing is near us but the Love itself that was before all worlds, and there is no doubt more, and no questioning more." Yet even as he thought it, the heart of the farmer, too, was full of the same longing after the heart of his boy who had never learned to cry *"Father!"*

Soon they sat down to their meal, the pleasantest of all meals, a farmhouse tea. Hardly anyone spoke, and no one missed the speech or was aware of the silence, until all at once Isy thought of her child and burst into tears. Then the mother, who sorrowed with such a difference and so much more bitter sorrow, knowing what she was thinking, rose from the table, came up behind her, and said, "Noo ye must jist come away wi' me, and I'll show ye yer bed, and leave ye there! Ye need not even say good-night to naebody—ye'll see the minister again in the mornin'."

She took Isy away, half-carrying her and half-leading her; for Marion, although no bigger than Isy, was much stronger and could have carried her easily.

That night both of the mothers slept well, and both dreamed of their mothers and of their children. But in the morning nothing remained of their two dreams except two hopes in the one Father.

When Isy entered the little parlor the next morning, she found that she had slept so long that breakfast was over, and the minister was sitting in the garden and the farmer was already busy in his field. Marion heard her come in and brought her breakfast, beaming with the ministering spirit of service. Thinking that she would eat it better if left to herself, she then went back to her work. In a few minutes, however, Isy joined her, and began at once to lend a helping hand.

"Hoot, hoot! my dear!" cried her hostess, "ye haena taken time enough to make a proper breakfast oot o' it! If ye dinna learn to eat, we'll never get any good o' ye!"

"I can't eat for gladness," returned Isy. "You're so good to me that I hardly dare think about it; it'll make me cry! Let me help you, ma'am, and I'll grow hungry enough by dinnertime."

Mrs. Blatherwick understood and said no more. She showed her what to do, and happy as a child, Isy came and went at her pleasant orders rejoicing. Had she started in life with less devotion, she might have fared better; but the end was not yet, and the end must be known before we dare judge: result explains history. For the present it is enough to say that, with the comparative repose of mind she now enjoyed, with the good food she had, and the wholesome exercise, for Mrs. Blatherwick took care she should not work too hard, with the steady kindness shown her, and the consequent growth of her faith and hope, Isy's light-heartedness and good looks soon began to return, so that the dainty little creature was soon both prettier and lovelier than before. At the same time her face and figure, her ways and motions, continued to mingle themselves so inextricably in Marion's mind with those of her departed daughter that before long she began to feel as if she would never be able to part with her. And it was not long either before she told herself that the remarkable girl was equal to anything that had to be done in the house; and that the experience of a day or two would make her capable of the work of the dairy as well. Thus, Isy and her mistress, for so Isy insisted on calling her, speedily settled into their new relationship as if the situation had been made for it.

It did sometimes cross the girl's mind with a sting of doubt, whether it was fair to hide from her new friends the full facts of her past, and the true relation in which she stood to them. But to quiet her conscience she had only to reflect that it was soley for the sake of the son they loved that she kept her silence. Further than James's protection she had no design, and cherished no scheme in her heart. The idea of influencing him in any way never once crossed the horizon of her thoughts. On the contrary, she was possessed by the notion that it was she who had done him a great wrong, and she shrank in horror from the danger of rendering it irretrievable. She had never thought the thing out as between her and him, never even said to herself that he too had been to blame. Her exaggerated notion of her own share of the fault had become so fixed in her mind that all she was capable of seeing was the possible injury she had done his prospects as a minister, which seemed to her a far greater wrong than any suffering of loss he might have brought upon her. For what was she beside him! What was the ruin of her life alongside the frustration of such magnificent prospects as his?

The sole alleviation of her misery in her mind was the comfort that thus far she seemed successfully to have avoided involving him in the results of her lack of self-restraint, results which she was sure had remained concealed from him to that day. In truth, never was a hidden wrong to a woman turned more eagerly and devotedly into loving service to the man's own parents. Many a time did the heart of James's mother, as she watched Isy's deft and dainty motions, regret that such a capable and love-inspiring girl should have made herself unworthy of her son. For despite what she regarded as the disparity of their social positions, she would gladly have welcomed Isy as a daughter had she but been spotless and fit to be loved by him.

In the evenings, when the work of the day was done, Isy would ramble about the moor in the lingering rays of the last of the sunset and in the now quickly shortening twilight which followed. In those lazy, gentle hours, so spiritual in their tone that they seemed to come straight from the eternal spaces where there is no remembering and no forgetting, where time and space are motionless, and the spirit is at rest, Isy first began to read with conscious understanding. For now for the first time she fell into the company of books—old-fashioned ones, no doubt, but perhaps therefore all the more fit for her in that she was an old-fashioned, gentle, naive, and thoughtful child. With one or two volumes in her hand, she would steal out of sight of the farm, and wrapped in the solitude of the moor would sit and read until at last the light could reveal not a single word more. She read some geometry, enjoyed rhetoric and poetry more, but liked natural history best of all, with its engravings of birds and animals, poor as they were.

In a garret over the kitchen, she also found an English translation of Klopstock's *Messiah*, a poem which, in the middle of the last and present century, caused a great excitement in Germany, and contributed much to the development of religious feeling in that country, where the slow-subsiding ripple of its commotion is possibly not altogether unfelt even at the present day. She read the volume through as she strolled in those twilights, not without risking falling over a bush or stone before practice taught her to see at once both the way for her feet over the moor and the way for her eyes over the printed page. The book both pleased and suited her, the parts that interested her most being those about the repentant angel, Abaddon, who haunted the steps of the Savior and hovered about the cross while he was crucified.

The great question with her for a long time was whether the Savior must not have forgiven him. By slow degrees it became at last clear to her that he who came but to seek and to save the lost could not have closed the door against one that sought to return to his faithfulness. It was not until she came to know the soutar, however, that at length she understood the tireless redeeming attribute of the love of the Father, who had sent men blind and stupid and ill-conditioned into a world where they had to learn almost everything.

There were some few books of a more theological sort, which happily she neither could understand nor was able to imagine she understood, and which therefore she instinctively refused as affording her no potential nourishment either for thought or feeling. There was, besides, Dr. Johnson's *Rasselas*, which mildly interested her, and a book called *Dialogues of Devils*, which she read eagerly. And thus, if indeed her ignorance did not grow much less as a result of these books, at least her knowledge of it grew a little greater, and that is certainly a great step in the direction of the truest kind of knowledge.

And all the time the conviction continued to grow upon her that she had been in that region before, and that in truth she could not be far from the spot where she had laid her child down and lost him.

17 / The Wisdom of the Wise Man_____

In the meantime the child was growing into a splendid boy, and was the delight of the humble dwelling to which Maggie had triumphantly borne him. But the mind of the soutar was busy in thought about how far their right in the boy approached the paternal. Were they justified in regarding him as their love-property before having made exhaustive inquiry as to who could possibly claim him? For nothing could liberate the finder of such a thing from the duty of restoring it upon demand, seeing that there could be no certainty that the child had been deliberately and finally abandoned.

Maggie, indeed, regarded the baby as hers absolutely by right of rescue. But her father asked himself whether they might not be depriving his mother of the one remaining link between her and humanity, and so abandoning her helpless to the Enemy. Surely to take and withhold from any woman her child must be to do what was possible toward dividing her from the unseen and eternal! And he saw that for the sake of the truth in Maggie, both she and he must make every possible attempt to restore the child to his mother.

So the next time his daughter brought the infant to the kitchen, her father, who sat as usual under the small window, to gather upon his work all the light to be had, turned his eyes with one quick glance at the child, and said, "Eh, the bonny, glad creature! Who can say that such as he, that haena his ain father and mother, mightna get frae the Lord himsel' a more particular and careful ootlook on life, if that be possible, than other bairns! I would like to believe that!"

"Eh, but ye think bonny, Father!" exclaimed Maggie. "Some say that such as he must turn oot anythin' but weel when they step oot into the world. Eh, but we must take care o' him, Father! But where *would* I be wi'oot you at my back?"

"And God at the back o' both!" rejoined the soutar. "I think the Almighty may hae a special diffeeculty wi' such as he, but none can judge anything or anybody till they see the final end o' it all. But I'm thinkin' it must aye be harder for one that hasna his ain mither to look to. Any other body, be she good as she may, must still be a makeshift mother. For one thing, he winna get the same natural discipline that every mither cat gives its kittens!''

"Maybe, maybe! I ken I couldna ever lay a finger upon the bonny creature mysel'!" said Maggie.

"There it is!" returned the father. "And we canna ken," he went on, "if we could expect much frae the wisdom o' the mither o' him if she had him. I doobt she might turn oot to be but a makeshift hersel'! There's many aboot him that'll be hard enough upon him, but none the wiser for that. Many a one'll look upon him as a bairn in whose existence God has had nae share. There's a heap o' mystery aboot all things, Maggie, from the very beginnin' to the very end. It may be that yon bairnie's in the worse danger just frae you and me, Maggie! We canna tell. Eh, but I wish his ain mither were given back to him! And who can tell but that she's needin' him worse than he's needin' her. 'Cause ye're no his ain mither, Maggie, an' I'm no his ain gran'father.''

With his words the adoptive mother broke into a howl. "Father, Father, ye'll break my heart by sayin' that!" she all but yelled.

She laid the child on the top of her father's hands as they were in the very act of drawing his waxed ends through a piece of leather, and thus changing him in an instant from cobbler to nurse, she bolted from the kitchen and up the little stair. There she threw herself on her knees by the bedside, seeking instinctively and unconsciously, the presence of him who sees in secret. But for a time she had nothing to say even to *him* and could only moan in the darkness that lay beneath her closed eyelids.

Suddenly she came to herself, and remembered that she too had abandoned the child and must go back to him.

But as she ran she heard loud noises of infantile jubilation. Reentering the kitchen she was at first amazed to see the soutar's hands moving persistently, if not quite so rapidly, as before with his work. The child hung at the back of her father's head, in the bend of the long jack-towel he had taken from behind the door, holding on by the gray hair of the back part of his head. There he tugged and crowed, while his caretaker bent over his labor, circumspect in every moment, never once forgetting the precious thing on his back, who was evidently delighted with his new style of being nursed, and only now and then made a wry face as some movement of the human machine too abrupt for his comfort. Evidently he took it all as intended solely for his pleasure.

Maggie burst out laughing through the tears that still filled her eyes, and the child, who could hear but not see her, began to cry a little. This roused the mother in her to a sense that he was being treated a bit too unceremoniously. She bound forward to liberate him, undid the towel, and seated herself with him in her lap. The grandfather, not sorry to be released, gave his shoulders a little relaxing shake, laughed an amused laugh, and set off boring and stitching and drawing at redoubled speed.

"Weel, Maggie," he said interrogatively, without looking up.

"I saw that ye was right, Father, and it set me cryin', sae that I forgot the bairn, and you too. Go on and say what ye think fit. It's all true."

"There's little left for me to say noo, lassie. Ye hae begun to say it yersel'. But believe me, though ye can never be the bairn's ain mither, *she* can never be to him the same as ye hae been already, whatever more or better may follow. The part ye hae chosen is good enough never to be taken frae ye—in this world or the next."

"Thank ye, Father, for that. I'll do for the bairn what I can without forgettin' he's no mine but anither's. I mustna take frae her what's her ain."

Whenever he was at his work, the soutar constantly tried to "get into his Lord's company," as he said—endeavoring to understand some saying of his, or to discover his reason for saying it when he did. Often he would ponder why God would allow this or that to take place in the world, for it was his house, where he was always present and always at work. He never doubted that when once a thing had taken place, that it was by his will it came to pass, but he saw that evil itself, originating with man or his deceiver, was often made to subserve the final will of the All-in-All. And he knew that much must first be set right before the will of the Father could be done in earth as it was in heaven.

Therefore, in any new development of feeling in his child, he could recognize the pressure of a guiding hand in the formation of her life's history, revealing what was in her, and making room for what was as yet undeveloped. Hence, he could love what his child was *becoming*, even without being able to see it in advance. Thus was he able to understand St. John's words: "Beloved, now are we the sons of God, and it doth not yet appear what we shall be, but we know that, when he shall appear, we shall be like him, for we shall see him as he is." For first and foremost, and deepest of all, he positively and absolutely believed in the man whose history is found in the Gospel—that is, he believed not only that such a man once was, and that every word he spoke was true, but he believed that the man was still in the world, and that every word he then spoke had always been, still was, and would always be true. Therefore, he also believed—which was the most important thing of all to both the Master and John MacLear, his disciple—that the chief end of his conscious life must be to live in the Lord's presence, and keep his affections ever afresh and constantly turning toward him, appealing to him for strength to believe and understand and then obey. Hence, every day he felt anew that he too was living in the house of God, among the things of the Father of Jesus.

The life influence of the soutar had already for some time been felt at Tiltowie. In a certain far-off way, men seemed to surmise what he was about, although they were incapable of estimating the nature or value of his pursuit of spiritual things. What their idea of him was may in a measure be gathered from the answer of the village fool when a passerby asked him, "Well, what's the soutar up to now?"

"Ow, as usual," answered the simpleton, "turnin' up ilka muckle stone to look for his Master beneath it!"

For in truth the cobbler did believe that the Lord of men was often walking to and fro in the earthly kingdom of his Father, watching what was going on there, and doing his best to bring it to its true and ideal condition. Never did John MacLear lift his eyes heavenward without a vague feeling that he might that very moment catch a sight of the glory of his coming Lord. If ever he fixed his eyes on the far horizon, it was never without receiving a shadowy suggestion that, like a sail towering over the edge of the world, the first great flag of the Lord's hitherward march might that moment be rising between earth and heaven. For certainly he would come unawares, and who then could tell what moment he might set his foot on the edge of the visible, and come out of the dark in which he had till that moment clothed himself as with a garment—to appear in the ancient glory of his transfiguration! Thus, he was ever on the watch. And yet even when deepest lost in such watching for his Savior, the lowest whisper of humanity was always loud enough to recall him to his "live work"—to wake him, that is to those around him, lest he should be found asleep to the needs of others at the moment of His Lord's coming. His was the same live readiness that had opened the ear of Maggie to the cry of the little one on the hillside. As his daily work was ministration to the weary feet of his Master's men, so was his soul ever awake to their sorrows and spiritual necessities.

"There's a whole world o' bonny work aboot me!" he would say. "I hae but to lay my hand to what's next me, and it's sure to be somethin' that wants doin'! I'm clean ashamed sometimes, when I wake up in the mornin', to find myself' doin' naething!"

Every evening while the summer lasted, he would go out alone for a walk, generally toward a certain wood near the town. For although it was of no great size and its trees were small, there lay the probability of escaping for a few moments from the eyes of men, and the chance of certain of another breed showing themselves.

"But I never cared that much aboot the angels," he once said to Maggie. "It's the perfect man, who was there wi' the Father afore ever an angel was heard tell o', that sends me upon my knees! When I see a man that but remin's me o' him, my heart rises up as if it would almost leave my body ahind it! Love's the law o' the universe, and it jist works amazin'!"

One day a man saw him approaching in the distance, and knowing he had not yet perceived his presence, lay down behind a great stone to watch "the mad soutar" go by in the hope of hearing him say something insane. As John came nearer, the silent observer saw his lips moving and heard sounds coming from them. But as he passed, nothing was audible but the same words repeated over several times, with the same expression of surprise and joy as if they were in response to something discovered for the first time:—"Eh, Lord! Eh, Lord, I see! I un'erstand!—Lord, I'm yer ain—to the very death!—

all yer ain!—Thy Father bless thee, Lord!—I ken ye care for naethin'
else!—Eh, but my heart's glad, Lord!''

Ever afterward the man spoke about the soutar with a respect that
resembled awe.

After that talk with her father about the child and his mother, a
certain silent change appeared in Maggie. People saw in her face an
expression which they took to resemble that of one whose child was
ill and was expected to die. But what Maggie was feeling was only
resignation to the will of her Lord: the child was not hers but the
Lord's, lent to her for a season. She must walk softly, doing everything for him as under the eye of her Master, who might at any
moment call to her, "Bring the child: I want him now!"

And before long she became as cheerful as before, although she
never quite lost the still, solemn look as of one in the eternal spaces
who was able to see beyond this world's horizon. She talked less
with her father, but at the same time she seemed to live closer to him.
Occasionally she would ask him to help her to understand something
he had said, but even then he would not always try to make it plain.

"I see, lassie," he might answer, "that ye're no just ready for it.
It's true enough, though, and the day must come when ye'll see the
thing itsel', and ken what it is, and that's the only way to get at the
truth o' it. In fact, to see a thing, and know the thing, and be sure
it's true, is all one and the same thing!" Such a word from her father
was always enough to still and content the girl.

Her delight in the child, instead of growing less, went on increas-
ing because of the awe rather than the dread of having at last to give
him up.

18 / The Boots

All this time young James Blatherwick remained moody, apparently sunk in contemplation, but in fact mostly brooding, and meditating on himself rather than on the truth. Sometimes he felt as if he were losing his power of thinking altogether—especially in the middle of the week when he sat down to try to find something to say on the next Sunday. He had completely lost interest in the questions that had occupied him while he was a student and had imagined himself in preparation for what he called the ministry—never thinking how one was to minister who had not yet learned to obey, and had never sought anything but his own glorification. It was indeed little wonder he should lose interest in a profession his heart took so little interest in. What pleasure could a man find in holy labor who did not indeed offer his pay to purchase the Holy Ghost, but instead offered all he knew of the Holy Ghost to purchase popularity? No wonder he should find himself at length in lack of talk to pay for his one most needful thing. He had always been more or less dependent on commentaries for the minimal food he provided: was it any wonder that his guests should show less and less appetite for the dinners that came from his hand.

The hungry sheep looked up and were not fed!

To have food to give them, he must think! To think, he must have peace! To have peace, he must forget himself! To forget himself, he must repent and walk in the truth! To walk in the truth, he must love God and his neighbor!

Even to have an interest in the dry bone of religious criticism and doctrinal discussion, which was all he could find in his larder, he must broil it—and so burn away every scrap of meat left on it in the slow fire of his intellect, now dull and damp enough from lack of noble purpose. His last relation to his work, his fondly cherished intellect, was departing from him to leave him nothing more than lord of a dustheap. In the unsavory mound he grubbed and nosed and

129

scraped about, but could not uncover a single fragment that smelt of true provender.

The morning of Saturday came, and he recognized with a burst of agonizing sweat that he dared not even face his congregation. He had not written one word to read to them, and extemporaneous utterance, from the vacancy of his mind and experience, was an impossibility to him. He could not even call up one meaningless phrase to articulate! He flung his concordance sprawling upon the floor, snatched up his hat and clerical cane, and hardly knowing what he was doing, presently found himself standing in front of the cobbler's door, where he had already knocked without the least idea of what he had come there seeking. The old parson, Mr. Pethrie, generally in a mood to quarrel with the soutar, had always walked straight into his workshop. But the new parson always waited on the doorstep for Maggie, whom he did not particularly want to see now, to admit him.

She opened the door wide before the minister had gathered his wits enough to know why he had come, or could think of anything to say. And the thought of the cobbler's deep-set black eyes about to fix themselves upon him put him in ever greater uneasiness than usual.

"Do you think your father would have time," he asked, "to measure me for a pair of boots?"

Blatherwick was very particular about his footgear, and before this had always fitted himself in Aberdeen. But he had finally learned that nothing he could buy there approached in quality, either of material or workmanship, what the soutar supplied to his poorest customer. For, while he would mend anything worth mending, he would never *make* anything inferior.

"'Deed, sir, he'll be glad an' prood to make ye as good a pair o' boots as he can make," answered Maggie. "Jist come in, an' let him ken what ye want. My bairn's cryin' and I must go to him; it's seldom he cries out."

The minister walked in at the open door of the kitchen and met the eyes of the cobbler.

"Welcome, sir!" said MacLear, and returned his eyes to his work.

"I would like you to make me a nice pair of boots," said the parson in as cheery a voice as he could muster. "Though I am afraid I am rather particular about the fit."

"And why shouldn't you be?" answered the soutar. "I'll do what I can anyway, I promise ye—but wi' more readiness than confidence as to the fit, for I canna profess a perfect fit the first time I make ye a pair o' the boots."

"Of course I should like to have them both neat and comfortable," said the parson.

"And sae would I. And when the time for a second pair comes, I'm sure I'd be closer to the ideal. But hoo will ye hae them made, sir?—I mean what sort o' boots would ye hae me make?"

"Oh, I leave that to you, Mr. MacLear!—a sort of half Wellington, I suppose—a neat pair of short boots."

"I un'erstand."

All of a sudden, moved by a sudden impulse that came from he knew not where, the minister began making conversation in an altogether new direction. "But tell me," he asked the cobbler, "what do you think of all this talk of the necessity of confessing one's sins to the priest; you must have read of it in the papers? I see they have actually gotten the miserable creature to confess to the murder of her little brother! Do you think they had any right to pressure her into such a confession? Remember the jury had already acquitted her."

"Has she really confessed? I hadn't read of it. I *am* glad o' it! Eh, the state o' that poor girl's conscience! It almost makes me cry to think o' it. With confession hope springs to life in the sin-oppressed soul. Eh, but it must be a gran' lightenin' thing to that poor girl! I'm right glad to hear o' it."

"I didn't know you favored the power and influence of the priesthood to such an extent, Mr. MacLear! We Presbyterian clergy are not in the habit of acting as detectives, taking it upon ourselves to act as agents of human justice. There is no one, whether he be guilty or not, who is not safe in what they tell us."

"As wi' any confessor, Catholic or Protestant," rejoined the soutar. "If I un'erstand what ye told me, it means that they persuaded the poor soul to confess her guilt, and so put hersel' safe in the hands o' God."

"And is that not to come between God and the sinner?"

"Perhaps—in order to bring them together; to persuade the sinner to the first step toward reconceeliation wi' God, and peace in his ain mind."

"That he could take without the intervention of the priest."

"Ay, but not wi'oot his ain consenting will. And in this case, she wouldna and didna confess wi'oot bein' persuaded by the priest to do it."

"They had no right to threaten her."

"I agree wi' ye there. If they did they were wrong. But in any case, they did the very best thing for her that could be done. For they did get her to confess—and sae cast frae her the horror o' carrin' aboot in her secret heart the knowledge o' an unforgiven crime. All Christians agree, dinna ye think, that to be forgiven, a sin must be confessed?"

"Yes, to God—that is enough. No mere man has a right to know the sins of his neighbor."

"Na even the man against whom the sin was committed?"

"Suppose the sin has never come to light, but remained hidden in the heart, is a man bound to confess it? For instance, is he bound to tell his neighbor that he used to hate him in his heart?"

"The time might come when to confess even that would ease a man's heart. But in such a case, the man's first duty, it seems to me, would be to watch for an opportunity o' doin' that neighbor a kin'-ness. That would be the death blow to the hatred in his heart. But where a man has done an act o' injustice, some wrong to his neighbor, he has no choice, it seems to me, but confess it: that neighbor is the one frae whom first he has to ask an' receive forgiveness. He alone can lift the burden o' guilt off the man. An' we mustna forget," ended the soutar, "hoo the Lord said that there's naethin' hidden but must come to the licht one day!"

Now what could have led the minister so near the truth of his own story, like the murdered who haunts the proximity of the loudest witness against his crime, except the will of God working in him to set him free, I do not know. But he went on, driven by an impulse he neither understood nor suspected.

"Suppose the thing wasn't known, and wasn't in the least likely to be known, and that the man's confession, instead of serving any good end, would only destroy his reputation and usefulness, bring bitter grief upon those who loved him, and nothing but shame to the one he had wronged—what would you say then? I am putting out an entirely imaginary case for the sake of argument only."

Eh, but I'm beginnin' to doobt yer imaginary case, thought the soutar to himself, hardly even daring to think his thought clearly. But to James he replied, "Even so, it seems to me the offender would hae to look aboot him for one to trust to whom he could reveal the whole affair, to get his help to see and do what's right. It makes a great difference to look at a thing through anither man's eyes, in the supposed light o' anither man's conscience. The wrong done may hae caused more evil or injustice than the man himsel' kens. And what's the reputation ye speak o', or the usefulness o' sich a man? Hoo can it be worth anythin'? Isna it all a lie? The only way for sich a man to destroy the hypocrisy is for him to cry oot to the world and his Maker, 'I'm a heepocrit! I'm no man, but, Lord, make a man oot o' me!' "

As the soutar spoke, overcome by sympathy with the sinner, whom he could not help suspecting was in bodily presence before him, the minister stood listening with a face pale as death.

Witnessing this change coming over his young friend, and moved powerfully by the compassion for him rising within him, the cobbler went on in an outburst of feeling:

"For God's sake, minister, if ye hae any such thing on ye mind, hurry an' be oot wi' it! I dinna say *to me*, but to somebody—to anybody! Make a clean breast o' it, afore the Adversary has ye by the throat!"

But with his words the pride of superiority in station and learning came again awake in the minister. How could a mere shoemaker, from whom he had just ordered a pair of shoes, take such a liberty! He drew himself up to his full lanky height, and replied— "I am not aware, Mr. MacLear, that I have given you any pretext for addressing me in such terms! I told you that I was merely asking about an imaginary case. You have shown me how unsafe it is to enter into a discussion with one of a limited education. It is my own fault, however, and I beg your pardon for having thoughtlessly led you into such a pitfall! Good morning to you!"

As he closed the door he congratulated himself on having so fortunately turned aside the course of a conversation whose dangerous drift he seemed now first to recognize. But he little realized how much he had already conveyed to the wide-eyed observation of one well-schooled in the symptoms of human unrest.

"I must watch my thoughts and word," he reflected, "lest they betray me!" And as he continued on his way he resolved to conceal himself yet more carefully from the one man in the place who could have helped cut for him the snare of the fowler.

"I was too hasty wi' him!" concluded the soutar to himself after his visitor had left. "But I think the truth has taken some grip o' him. His conscience is wakin' up, I fancy, and growlin' a bit. And where that tyke has once taken hold, he's no ready to loosen or let go! We must jist lie quiet a bit and see. His hoor will come!"

The minister was one who turned pale when angry, and thus walked home with such a white face that a woman who met him said to herself, "I wonder what can ail the minister, bonny lad! He's lookin' as scared as a corpse! I doobt that fule body the soutar's been angerin' him wi' his talk!"

Despite his anger, the first thing he did when he reached the manse was to turn to one of the chapters he thought the soutar had vaguely quoted from, and which, through all his irritation had strangely enough, remained vaguely in his memory. But the passage suggested nothing out of which he could fabricate a sermon, and he was left no nearer that end than before.

How could it be otherwise with a heart that was quite content to have God no nearer than a merely adoptive Father? His interview with the cobbler had rendered the machinery of his thought factory no fitter than before for weaving a tangled wisp of loose ends into the homogeneous web of a sermon. And at last he was driven to his old stock of carefully preserved preordination sermons, where he was unfortunate enough to make choice of the one least of all fitted to awake comprehension of interest in his audience.

His selection made, and the rest of the day thus cleared for inaction, he sat down and wrote a letter. Ever since his fall he had been successfully practicing the art of throwing occasional morsels toward his conscience, which was more clever in catching them than they were in quieting the said howler's restiveness. This letter was the sole result of his talk with John MacLear. It was addressed to one of his divinity classmates, and in it he asked incidentally whether his old friend had ever heard anything of the little girl—he could just remember her name and the pretty face of her—Isy, general helper to her aunt's lodgers in the Canongate, of whom he had been one. He had often wondered, he said, what had become of her, for he had been almost in love with her for a time. I don't doubt that the inquiry was the merest pretense with the sole object of deceiving himself into the notion of his having at least made one attempt to discover Isy's whereabouts.

His friend forgot to answer the question, and James Blatherwick never alluded to his having put it to him.

19 / The Sermon

Never did a Sunday dawn more wretched upon a human soul. At least James did not have to climb into his watchman's tower, the pulpit, without some pretense of a proclamation to give. But on that very morning, his father had put the mare between the shafts of the gig to drive his wife to Tiltowie and their son's church, instead of the nearer and more accessible one in the next parish, where they usually went.

It was hardly surprising that they should find themselves so dissatisfied with the spiritual food set before them that they wished they had remained at home. The moment the service was over, Mr. Blatherwick felt inclined to climb back into the gig and return at once without even waiting to speak with his son. He had nothing to say about the sermon that would be pleasant either for his son or his wife to hear. But Marion argued with him, almost to the point of anger, and Peter was compelled to yield. Thus they waited, Peter almost sullenly, in the churchyard for the minister's appearance.

"Weel, Jamie," said his father, shaking hands with him, "yon was some hardened porridge ye gave us this mornin'!—an' the meal itsel' was both auld an' sour."

The mother gave her son a pitiful smile, as if to soften her husband's severity, but she said no word. Haunted by the taste of failure the sermon had left in his own mouth, and troubled as well by the self-conscious waking of self-recognition, James could hardly look his father in the face. He felt as if he had been rebuked by him, as though he were still a child, in front of his whole congregation.

"Father," he replied in a tone of some injury, "you do not know how difficult it is to preach a fresh sermon every Sunday!"

"Call ye that fresh, Jamie? To me it was like the moldy husks o' the half-famished swine! Man, I wish such provender would drive ye where there's better food, an' to spare! Yon was lumps o' brose in a pig-wash o' stourum! I'd think ye'd ken the differ' atween sich like an' true food!''

James made a wry face, and the sight of his annoyance broke the ice gathering over the well-spring in his mother's heart. Tears rose in her eyes, and for one brief moment she saw the minister again as her own tiny bairn. But he gave her no filial response. His own ambition, and his desire for the praise of men, had blocked in him the movements of the divine and corrupted the wholesomest of his feelings. This combined with his father's comments caused him to welcome freely the false conviction that his parents had never had any sympathy with him or cared the least about his preaching. All reacted together in a sudden flow of resentment and a thickening of the ice between them. Some fundamental shock would be necessary to unsettle and dislodge that deeply rooted, overmastering ice over his innermost being, if ever his wintered heart was to feel the power of a reviving spring!

The threesome family stood in helpless silence for a few moments, and then the father said to the mother, "Weel, I doobt we must be settin' oot for home, Marion.''

"Will you not come to the manse and have something to eat before you go?'' asked James, not without anxiety that his housekeeper should be taken by surprise, and their acceptance of his invitation annoy her. He lived in constant dread of offending his housekeeper.

"Na, thank ye,'' returned his father, "it would likely taste o' blown dust.''

It was a rude remark. But Peter was not in a kind mood, and when love itself is unkind, it is apt to be burning and bitter and merciless.

Marion burst into tears. James turned away, and walked home with a gait of wounded dignity. Peter went hastily toward the churchyard gate, to interrupt with the bit his mare's leisurely feed of oats. Marion saw his hands tremble pitifully as he put the headstall over the creature's ears, and reproached herself that she had given him such a cold-hearted son. In a helpless way, she climbed into the gig and sat waiting for her husband.

They drove away from the tombs of the church graveyard, but they carried the feeling of death with them. Neither spoke a word all the way. Not until she was dismounting at their own door, did the mother venture her sole remark, "Eh, sirs!" It meant a world of unexpressed and inexpressible misery. She went straight up to the little garret where she kept her Sunday bonnet, and where she said her prayers when she was in special misery. After a while she came down to her bedroom, there washed her face, and sadly prepared for a hungerless encounter with the dinner Isy had been getting ready for them—hoping to hear something about the sermon, perhaps even some little word about the minister himself.

But Isy, too, had to share in the disappointment of that glorious Sunday morning. Not a word passed between her master and mistress. Their son was called pastor of the flock, but he was rather the porter of the sheepfold than the shepherd of the sheep. He was very careful that the church should be clean and properly swept, and sometimes even painted, but about the temple of the Holy Spirit, the hearts of his sheep, he knew nothing.

The gloom of his parents, their sense of failure and loss, grew and deepened all the dull hot afternoon, until it seemed almost to pass their power of endurance. At last, however, it abated, as does every pain, for life is at its root: thereto ordained, it slew itself by exhaustion. But even though she felt better by degrees, the mother could only think of the coming of another new day that would bring the old trouble back upon her—the gnawing, sickening pain that she was childless—her daughter gone and no son left. Nonetheless, however, when the new day came, it brought with it its own new possibility of living yet one day more.

But their son the minister was far more to be pitied than those whom he gave misery. All night long he slept with a sense of ill-usage sublying his consciousness and dominating his dreams. But when the morning broke there came the thought into his brain that possibly he had not acted in the most seemly fashion when he turned and left his father and mother in the churchyard. Of course they had not treated him well. But what would his congregation have thought to see him leave them as he did—and some of them might have been lingering in the churchyard? His only thought, however, was not toward repentance, but to take precautions against their natural judgment of his behavior.

After breakfast, as custom was every Monday morning, he set our for what he called a quiet stroll. But his thoughts kept returning, ever with fresh resentment, to the soutar's insinuation two days before.

Suddenly the face of Maggie arose before him, quickly displacing the phantasm of her father. His thoughts came before he could stop them, and suddenly he was asking himself the question, "What was the *real* history of the baby on whom she spent such an irrational amount of devotion?" The soutar's tale of her finding him was too apocryphal! Might not Maggie have made a moral slip? Or why should the pretensions of the soutar be absolutely trusted? With the idea arose in him a certain satisfaction in the possible prospect of learning that this man, so ready to believe evil of his neighbor, had not succeeded in keeping his own house undefiled. He tried to rebuke himself the next moment, it is true, for having harbored even a moment's satisfaction in the wrongdoing of another: it was unbefitting the pastor of a Christian flock. But the thought came and went, and he took no conscious trouble to try to cast it out. When he returned from his walk, he put a question or two to his housekeeper about the child, but she only smiled faintly and shook her head knowingly, as if she knew more than she chose to tell.

After his two o'clock dinner, he thought it would be Christian-like to forgive his parents and call at Stonecross: the action would tend to wipe out any undesirable offense on the minds of his parents, and also to prevent any gossip that might injure him in his sacred profession. He had not been to see them for a long time, and though such visits gave him no satisfaction, he never dreamed of attributing it to his own lack of cordiality. But he judged it prudent to avoid any appearance of neglect, and therefore thought that in the future it might be his duty to attempt a hurried call about once a month. He excused himself for his infrequency in the past because of the distance and his not being a good walker. And even after he had made up his mind, he was in no haste to set out, but had a long snooze in his armchair first. So it was almost evening before he climbed the hill and came in sight of the low gable behind which he was born.

Isy was in the garden gathering up the linen she had spread out to dry on the gooseberry bushes. The moment his head came in sight at the top of the brae, she knew him at once, and stooping behind the gooseberries, she fled to the back of the house, and then away to the moor on the other side. James saw the white flutter of the sheet, but nothing of the hands that took it. He had heard that his mother had a nice young woman to help her in the house, but he had so little interest in home affairs that the news had waked no curiosity in him.

Ever since she came to Stonecross, Isy had been on the lookout lest James should unexpectedly come upon her, and be surprised into an involuntary disclosure of his relation to her. Despite her long hope of seeing him again, she remained vigilant, for the longer he delayed, the more certain it became that he must soon appear. She did not intend to avoid him altogether, only to take heed not to startle him into any recognition of her in the presence of his mother. But when she saw him approaching the house, her courage failed her, and she fled to the fields to avoid the danger of betraying both herself and him. In truth, she was ashamed of meeting him, in her imagination feeling guilty and exposed to his just reproaches. All the time he remained with his mother, she kept watching the house, not once showing herself until he was gone. Then she would reappear as if just returned from the moor, where Mrs. Blatherwick imagined her still indulging the hope of finding her baby. Her mistress had come more and more to doubt the existence of the child, taking the supposed fancy for nothing but a half-crazy survival from the time of her insanity before the Robertsons found her.

The minister made a comforting peace with his mother, telling her a part of the truth, namely that he had been much out of sorts during the week and quite unable to write a new sermon. At the last he had been driven to take an old one, and so hurriedly that he had failed to recall correctly the subject and nature of it. He had actually begun to read it, he said, before discovering that it was altogether unsuitable—at which very moment, fatally for his equanimity, he saw his parents in the congregation. He was so dismayed that he could not recover his self-possession, and from all this had come his apparent lack of cordiality. It was a lame, yet somewhat plausible excuse, and served to silence for the moment, if not to satisfy, his mother's heart. His father was out-of-doors, and James did not see him.

20 / The Passing

As time went on, the terror of discovery grew rather than abated in the mind of the minister. He could not tell why it should be so, for no news of Isy had reached him. In his quieter moments, he felt almost certain that she could not have passed so completely out of his horizon if she were still in the world. It was when he was most persuaded of this that he was able to live most comfortably and forget the past, of which he was unable to recall any portion with satisfaction. The darkness and silence left over it by his unrepented offense, gave it, in the retrospect of his thoughts, a threatening aspect—out of which any moment might burst the hidden enemy, the thing that might be known, and more not be known! He managed to derive a feeble cowardly comfort in the reflection that he had done nothing to hide the miserable fact. He even persuaded himself that if he could he *would* not now do anything further to keep it secret. He would leave all that to Providence, which seemed till now to have wrought on his behalf. He would but keep a silence that no gentleman must break! Besides, who had any claim to know a mere passing fault? Why should there be any call for a confession, about which the soutar had carried on so foolishly?

If the secret should threaten to creep out, he would not, he flattered himself, move a finger to keep it hidden. On the contrary, that moment he would disappear in some trackless solitude, rejoicing that he had nothing left to wish hidden. As to the charge of hypocrisy that was sure to follow, he was innocent. He had never said anything he did not believe! He had never once posed as a man of Christian experience—like the cobbler, for instance! He had simply been overtaken in a fault, which he had never repeated, never would repeat, and which he was willing to atone for in any way he could.

On the following Saturday, the soutar was hard at work all day long on the new boots the minister had ordered, which indeed he had almost forgotten in his anxiety for the young man. For MacLear was now thoroughly convinced that some hidden offense lay deep within the minister's mind. He was anxious to finish the boots so that he might take them to him that same night, and possibily find an opportunity to say something further in the way of helping point the man toward returning health. For nothing attracted the soutar more than an opportunity of doing anything to lift from a human soul, even but a single fold of the darkness that covered it, and so let the light nearer to the troubled heart.

As to what it might be that was harassing the minister's soul, he sternly repressed in himself all curiosity. He had no particular desire that James should unburden himself to him, but hoped what he said would send him seeking counsel from someone who could help him, and that in time they would gradually be able to resume their friendly relationship with each other. For somehow there was that in the gloomy parson which attracted the cheery and hopeful cobbler, and he hoped the young man's trouble might yet prove to be the hunger of his heart after a spiritual food he had not yet begun to find. He might not yet have understood, the soutar thought, the good news about God—that he was just what Jesus was to those who saw the glory of God in his face. The minister could not, he thought, have learned much about the truth concerning his heavenly Father, for it seemed to wake in him no gladness, no power of life, no strength to *be*. For *him* Christ had not risen, but lay wrapped in his death clothes. So far as James's experience was concerned, the larks and the angels must all be mistaken in singing as they did! For there was no power of the resurrection in his life!

Late that night, so late in fact that the cobbler worried that the housekeeper had probably retired for the night, he rang the bell of the manse door. And indeed it was the minister himself who answered the door, to see MacLear on the other side of the threshold, with the new boots in his hand.

Since their last encounter, the minister had come to feel that the soutar must suspect him of something; otherwise, why would he have said what he did? He was now bent on removing any negative impression his words might have had. Therefore he wanted to appear to be harboring no offense over his parishioner's last words, and so obliterate any suggestion of needed confession on his own part. Thus he now addressed him almost lightly, with a tone very different from his usually gloomy spirit.

"Oh, MacLear," he said, "I am glad to see you have just managed to escape breaking the Sabbath! You have had a close shave! There are only ten minutes more to the awful midnight hour!"

"I doobt, sir, it would hae broken the Sabbath worse to fail in my word wi' my work on yer boots," returned the soutar.

"Ah well, we won't argue about it. But if we were inclined to be strict, the Sabbath began some"—here he looked at his watch—"some five and three-quarters hours ago; that is, at six of the clock, the evening of Saturday."

"Hoot, minister, ye ken ye're wrong there! for Jew-wise, it began at six o'clock on the Friday night! But ye hae made it plain frae the pulpit that ye hae no superstition aboot the first day o' the week, which alone has anythin' to do wi' us Christians. I for one confess nae obligation but to drop workin', and sit doon wi' clean hands, or as clean as I can weel make them, to the spiritual table o' my Lord, where I aye try as well to wear a clean and cheerful face—that is, sae far as the sermon will permit. For isna it the bonny day when the Lord would hae us sit doon and eat wi' himsel', who made the heavens and the earth, and the waters under the earth that hold it up. And will he, upon this day, at the last gran' marriage feast, poor oot the bonny red wine, and say, 'Sit ye doon, bairns, and take o' my best!' "

"Ay, ay, MacLear, that's a fine way to think of the Sabbath!" rejoined the minister, "and the very way I am in the habit of thinking of it myself! I'm greatly obliged to you for bringing home my boots. Come in and put them there on that bench in the window. It's about time we were all going to bed, I think—especially myself, tomorrow being sermon-day."

The soutar went home and to his bed, sorry that he had said nothing.

The next evening he listened to the best sermon he had yet heard from that pulpit—a summary of the facts bearing on the resurrection of our Lord. A large part of the congregation, however, was anything but pleased, for the minister had admitted the impossibility of reconciling, in every particular detail, the differing account of the doings and seeings of those who witnessed it.

"—As if," said the soutar, "the Lord wasna to show himsel' openly till all that saw the thing were agreed to their recollection o' what folk had reported!"

He went home edified and uplifted by his fresh contemplation of the story of his Master's victory. Thank God, he thought, his pains were over at last, and through death he was Lord forever over death and evil, over pain and loss and fear. He was Lord also of all thinking and feeling and judgment, able to give repentance and restoration, and to set right all that self-will had set wrong.

So greatly did the heart of his humble disciple rejoice him that he scandalized the reposing Sabbath-street by breaking out, as he went home, into a somewhat unmelodious song, "They are all gone down to hell with the weapons of their war!" to a tune nobody knew but himself, and which he could never have sung again. "O Faithful and True," he broke out again as he reached his own house; but stopped suddenly, saying, "Tut, tut, the folk'll think I hae been drinkin'!—Eh," he continued to himself as he went in, "if I might but once hear the name that no man kens but himsel'!"

The next day he was very tired and could get through but little work. So on the next he decided to take a little holiday. Therefore he put a large piece of oatcake in his pocket, told Maggie he was going for a walk in the hills, and then disappeared with a single backward look and lingering smile.

After walking some distance in quiet peace, and having for a long while met no one—by which he meant that no special thought had arisen in his mind, he turned and headed toward Stonecross. He had known Peter Blatherwick for many years, and honored him as one in whom there was no guile, and now suddenly the desire came upon him to visit him.

He knocked on the door, and to his surprise the farmer himself came to answer it, and stood there in silence with a look that seemed to say, "I know you, but what can you be wanting with me?" His face was troubled, and looked not only sorrowful, but scared as well. Usually ruddy with health, and calm with contentment, it was now very pale and white, and seemed, as he held the door-handle without a word of welcome, that of one aware of something unseen behind him.

"What ails ye, Mr. Blatherwick?" asked the soutar in a voice of sympathetic anxiety. "I hope there's naething come o'er the mistress."

"An, thank ye; she's very weel. But a dreadful thing has jist befallen us. Only an hour ago oor Isy—the girl we brought into oor home not so long ago—jist dropped doon dead. Ye would hae thought she was shot wi' a gun. The one moment she was standin' talkin' wi' her mistress in the kitchen, and the next she was in a heap on the floor!—But come in, come in!"

"Eh, the bonnie lassie!" cried the shoemaker, making no move to enter. "I remember her weel, though I saw her only once—a fine delicate picture o' a lassie, that looked up at ye as if she made ye kindly welcome to anything she could give or get for ye! Was she ailin'?"

"No so bad! Though she was weak all along, at death's very door when Mister Robertson found her in Aberdeen. But I had thought she was comin' back to her health right weel. But we'll see her no more till the earth gives up her dead. The wife's in there wi' what's left o' her, cryin' as if she would cry her eyes oot. Eh, but she loved her!—Doon she dropped, and never a moment to say her prayers!"

"That matters no much—not a hair, in fact!" returned the soutar. "It was the Father o' her that took her, and none other. He wanted her home; and he's no one to do anything ill, or at the wrong moment! If a minute more had been any good to her, don't ye think she would hae had that minute?"

"Willna ye come in and see her? Some fowk canna bide to look upon the dead, but ye're no one o' such."

"No, I darena be such a one. I'll willin'ly go wi' ye to look upon the face o' one that's won through."

"Come then, and maybe the Lord'll give ye a word o' comfort for the mistress, for she's takin' on terrible aboot her. It breaks my heart to see her."

"The heart o' both king and cobbler's in the hand o' the Lord," answered the soutar solemnly, "and if my heart hears anything, my tongue'll be ready to speak the same."

He followed the farmer—who walked softly, as if he feared disturbing the sleeper upon whom even the sudden silences of the world would break no more.

Mr. Blatherwick led the way to the parlor, and through it to a little room behind which they used as the guest chamber. There, on a little white bed with white curtains drawn all the way back, lay the form of Isobel. The eyes of the soutar, in whom had lingered yet still a small hope, at once revealed that he saw she was indeed gone to return no more. Her lovely little face, although its eyes were closed, was even lovelier than before. But her arms and hands lay straight by her sides; their work was gone from them and nothing was left them to do. No voice would call her anymore; she might sleep on and take her rest.

"I had but to lay them straight," sobbed her mistress. "Her eyes she had closed herself. Eh, but she *was* a bonny lassie—and a good one!—hardly less than a bairn to me!"

"And to me as weel!" added Peter, with a choked sob.

"And no once had I paid her a penny in wages!" cried Marion, with sudden remorseful memory, as if she had done the girl a great wrong.

"She never wanted it—and never will noo," said her husband.

"Eh, she was a decent, right lovable creature!" cried Marion. "She never *said* anythin' to judge by, but I had a hope that she may hae been one o' the Lord's ain."

"Is that all ye can say, mem?" interposed the soutar. "Surely ye wouldna dare imagine that she dropped oot o' *his* hands!"

"Na," returned Marion. "But I would right fain ken her fair into them! For who is there to assure us o' her faith in the atonement?"

"'Deed, I kenna, and I carena, mem! I hope she had faith in naething but the Lord himsel'! Alive or dead, we're in *his* hands who died for us, revealin' his Father to us," said the soutar. "And if she didna ken him afore, she will noo! The holy one will be wi' her in the dark, or whatever comes!—O God, hold up her head, and let not the waters go ower her!"

So-called theology tried to rise, dull and rampant and indignant, in the minds of both Peter and Marion. But the solemn face of the dead kept them from dispute, and Love was ready to hope, if not quite to believe. Nevertheless, to those guileless souls, the words of

the soutar sounded like blasphemy: was not her fate already settled—
to the one side of eternity or the other—and forever to remain the
same? Had not death in a moment turned her into an immortal angel,
or an equally immortal devil? Yet how could they argue the possibility, with the peaceful face before them, that as loving and gentle
as she was, she could not be as utterly indifferent to the heart of the
living God as if he had never created her—nay, even had become
hateful to him!

No one spoke, and after gazing on the dead for a while, prayer
overflowing his heart but never reaching his lips, the soutar placed
in her hands a rose that he had picked on his walk, turned slowly and
departed without a word.

Just about the time he reached his own door, he met the minister,
and told him of the sorrow that had befallen his parents, adding that
it was plain they were sorely in need of his sympathy. Although James
thought it unusual that they would be so troubled by the death of a
mere servant, he was yet roused by the tale to do the duty of his
profession. Though his heart had never yet drawn him either to the
house of mourning or the house of joy, he judged that it would be
becoming of him to pay another visit to Stonecross, though he did
think it unfortunate that he should have to go again so soon. It pleased
the soutar, however, to see him turn about and start for the farm with
a quicker stride than he had used since his return to Tiltowie.

James had not the slightest forboding of whom he was about to
see in the arms of death. But even had he had some feeling of what
was awaiting him, I dare not even conjecture the mood with which
he would have approached the house—whether one of conscience or
of relief. But utterly unconscious of the discovery toward which he
was rushing, he hurried on, with almost a faint sense of pleasure at
the thought of having to expostulate with his mother upon the waste
of such an unnecessary expenditure of feeling. Toward his father, he
was aware of a more active feeling of disapproval, not an altogether
unusual thing. There are many in the world who have not yet learned
to love, still less to trust their parents. James Blatherwick was one
of those whose sluggish natures require, for the melting of their
stubbornness and their remolding into forms of strength and beauty,
such a concentration of the love of God that it becomes a consuming
fire.

21 / The Vigil

Night had fallen by the time James reached the farm. The place was silent, its doors were all shut, and when he went inside not a soul was to be seen. No one came to meet him, for no one had even thought of him, and certainly no one, except it were the dead, desired his coming.

He went into the parlor, and there, from the dim chamber beyond whose door stood open, appeared his mother. Her heart big with grief, she clasped him in her arms and laid her face against his chest. Higher than that she could not reach, and nearer than his breastbone she could not get to him. No endearment had ever been natural to James. He had never encouraged or missed any, and did not know how to receive it when it was offered.

"I am distressed, Mother," he began, "to see you so upset. I cannot help thinking such a display of feeling to be unnecessary. If I may say so, it seems unreasonable. You cannot, in such a brief period as this new maid of yours has spent with you, have developed such an affection for her. The young woman can hardly be a relative. The suddenness of the occurrence, of which I only heard from my shoemaker, MacLear, must have played terribly upon your nerves! Come, come, dear Mother, you must compose yourself! It is quite unworthy of you to yield to such an unnatural and uncalled-for grief. Surely a Christian like you should meet such a thing with calmness. Was it not Schiller who said, 'Death cannot be an evil, for it is universal'?"

During this foolish speech, the gentle woman had been restraining her sobs behind her handkerchief. But as she heard her son's cold commonplaces, it was perhaps a little wholesome anger that roused her and made her able to speak.

"Ye didna ken her, laddie," she cried, "or ye would never say such a thing! But I doobt if ever ye could hae come to ken her as she was—such a bonny, hearty sowl as once dwelt in yon white-faced, patient thing lying in the room there—with the sting oot o' her heart

151

at last, and left the sharper in mine! But me and yer father, we loved her. She was more a daughter than a servant to us, wi' a lovin' kindness no to be looked for frae any son!—Jist go into the room there, if ye will, and ye'll see what'll maybe soften yer heart a bit, and let ye understand the heartache that's come to the two old fowk ye never cared much aboot!''

James was bitterly aggrieved by this personal remark by his mother. What had *he* ever done to offend her? Had he not always behaved himself properly toward them? What right had she to say such things to him! Had he not fulfilled the expectation with which his father sent him to college? Had he not gained a position whose reflected splendor crowned them the parents of James Blatherwick? She showed him none of the consideration or respect he had so justly earned but never demanded!

He rose suddenly, and with never a thought other than to get out of his mother's presence for a moment so as to make his displeasure clear, stalked heedlessly into the presence of the more heedless dead.

The night had fallen, but the small window of the room looked westward and a bar of golden light yet lay like a resurrection stone over the spot where the sun was buried. A pale, sad gleam, softly vanishing, hovered, hardly rested, upon the lovely, still, unlooking face that lay white on the scarcely whiter pillow. For an instant, the sharp, low light blinded him a little, yet he seemed to have something before him not altogether unfamiliar, giving him a suggestion as of something he had once known, perhaps ought now to recognize, but had forgotten. The reality of it seemed to be obscured by the strange autumnal light entering almost horizontally.

Concluding himself oddly affected by the sight of the room he had always regarded with some awe in his childhood, and had not set foot in for a long time, he drew a little nearer to the bed in order to look closer at the face of this servant whose loss was causing his mother such an unreasonably poignant sorrow.

The sense of something known grew stronger. Yet still he did not fully recognize the death-changed countenance, although he was sure that he *had* seen that still and quiet face before. If she would but open those eyes for a moment, he was certain he should know at once who it was.

Then the true suspicion flashed upon him: Good God! *could it be* the dead Isy?

Of course not! It was the merest illusion! a nonsensical fancy caused by the irregular mingling of the light and darkness. In the daytime he would never have been so fooled by his imagination! Yet even as he said this to himself, he stood as one transfixed, with his face leaning close down staring upon the face of the dead. It was only like her; it could not be the same face! Still he could not turn and go from it! And as he stared, the dead face seemed to come nearer him through the darkness, growing more and more like the only girl he had ever, though then only in fancy, loved. If it was not she, how could the dead look so like the living he had once known? At length what doubt was left changed suddenly to an assurance that it must be she. And with the realization, he breathed a sigh of such false relief as he had not known since his sin, and with that sigh he left the room. He passed his mother, who still wept in the now deeper dusk of the parlor, made the observation that there was no moon and that it would be quite dark before he reached home, and with that bade her good-night and went out.

Peter had been unable to sit any longer inactive and had some time before gone out to the stable. However, when he had been foiled in the attempt to occupy himself, he came back into the house and sat down by his wife. She began to talk about the funeral preparations and the people they should invite. But such sorrow overtook him afresh, that even his wife, inconsolable as she was herself, was surprised at the depth of his grief for one who was no relative. To him it seemed indelicate, almost heartless that she should talk so soon of burying the dear one but just gone from their sight.

"What's the hurry?" he expostulated. "Isna there time enough to think aboot all that in the morn? Let my sowl rest a moment wi' death, and dinna talk more aboot yer funeral. 'Sufficient to the day,' ye ken."

"Eh, Peter, I'm no like you. When the sowl's gone, I can take no contentment in the presence o' the poor worthless body, lookin' what it never more can be. But be it as ye will, my man. It's a sore heart ye hae as well as mine, and we must bear one anither's burdens. The dear girl may lie as we hae laid her the night through. There's little enough to be done for her anyway; she's a bonny clean corpse as ever was, and may weel lie a few days afore we put her away. I dinna think there's need to watch her; no dogs or cats'll come near her. I hae aye wondered what for fowk would sit up wi' the dead, yet I remember weel that they did it in the old times."

In this alone she showed that the girl she lamented was not her own, for when her daughter died, her body was never for a moment left with the eternal spaces, as if she might wake and be terrified to find herself alone. Then, as if God had forgotten them, they went to bed without saying their usual prayers together. I fancy the visit of her son had been to Marion like the chill of a wandering iceberg.

In the morning the farmer was as usual up first, and went into the death-chamber and down by the side of the bed. And as he sat looking at the white face, he became aware of the faintest possible tinge of color on the lips. Were his eyes deceiving him? It must be his fancy, or at best an accident without significance—for he had heard of such a thing. Still, even if his eyes were deceiving him, he could not think of hiding away such death out of sight. The merest counterfeit of life was too sacred for burial. This might have been just how the little daughter of Jairus looked when the Lord took her by the hand before she arose! It was no wonder Peter could not entertain the thought of her immediate burial. They must at least wait some sign, some unmistakable proof of change begun.

Therefore, instead of going outside into the yard to set in motion the preparations necessary for the coming harvest, Peter sat on with the dead: He could not leave her until his wife should come to take his place and keep her company. He brought a Bible from the next room, sat down again and waited beside her. In doubtful, timid, tremulous hope—a mere sense of scarcely possible possibility, he waited for what he could not consent to believe he waited for. He would not deceive himself nor raise his wife's hopes. He would say nothing, but wait to see how it appeared to her. He would ask her no leading question, but merely watch for any look of surprise she might betray.

By and by his wife appeared, gazed a moment on the dead, looked pitifully in her husband's face, and went out again.

"She sees naething!" said Peter to himself. "I'll go to my work.

But I winna hae her laid aside afore I'm a good bit surer o' what she is—a livin' sowl or a dead body.''

With a sad sense of vanished self-delusion, he rose and went out. As he passed through the kitchen, his wife followed him to the door.

"Ye'll send a message to the carpenter aboot a coffin today?" she whispered.

"I'm not likely to forget," he answered; "but there's nae hurry, seein' there's no life concerned.''

"Na, none; the more's the pity," she answered; and Peter knew, with a glad relief, that his wife was coming to herself from the terrible blow.

She sent their hired man to the Cormack's cottage to tell Eppie to come to her.

The old woman came, heard what details there were to the sad story, shook her head mournfully, and found nothing to say. But together they set about preparing the body for burial. That done, the mind of Mrs. Blatherwick was at ease, and she sat down expecting the visit of the carpenter. But he did not come.

On the Thursday morning the soutar came to inquire about his friends at Stonecross, and Mrs. Blatherwick gave him a message to Willie Webster, the carpenter, to see about the coffin.

But catching sight of the farmer in the yard, the soutar went and had a talk with him. The result was that he took no message to Willie Webster, and when Peter went in to his midday dinner, he still said there was no hurry. Why should she be so anxious to heap earth over the dead? In his heart of hearts he still fancied he saw the same possible color in Isy's cheek, the same that is in the heart of the palest blush-rose, which is either glow or pallor as you choose to think it. So the first days of Isy's death passed, and still she lay in state, ready for the grave, but unburied.

A good many of the neighbors came to see her, and were admitted where she lay. Some of them warned Marion that when the change came, it would come suddenly. But still Peter would not hear of her being buried. By this time Marion had come to see, or to imagine with her husband that she saw the color. So each in turn, they kept watching her. Who could tell but that the Lord might be going to work a miracle for them, and was not in the meantime only trying them, to see how long their patience and hope would endure.

22 / The Waking

The report spread through the neighborhood and reached Tilto-wie, where it speedily pervaded street and lane: "The lass at Stone-cross is lying dead, and looking as alive as ever!" From all quarters the people went crowding to see the strange sight, and would have overrun the house had they not been met with less than a cordial reception: the farmer set men at every door and would admit no one. Angry and ashamed, they all turned and went—except for a few of the more inquisitive, who continued lurking about in the hope of hearing something to carry home and enlarge upon their gossip.

The minister insisted on disbelieving the whole thing, and yet he could not help being very uncomfortable by the report. Always a foe to the supernatural, in his own mind silently questioning the truth of the biblical record of miracles in general, he still found himself haunted by a fear which he dare not formulate. Of course, whatever might be taking place, it could be no miracle, but the mere natural effect of natural causes! Nonetheless, however, did he dread what might happen. He feared Isy and what she might say.

For a time, therefore, he dared not go near the place. The girl might be in a trance. She might suddenly revive and call out his name! She might even reveal all! What if, indeed, she were even being now kept alive to tell the truth and disgrace him before the whole world! Horrible as was the thought, might it not be a good idea, in view of the possibility of her revival, for him to be present to hear anything she might say, so he could take precaution against it? He decided, therefore, to go to Stonecross and ask about her, heartily hoping to find her undoubtedly and irrecoverably dead.

In the meantime, Peter had been growing more and more ex-pectant, and had nearly forgotten all about the coffin, when a fresh rumor came to the ears of William Webster that the young woman at Stonecross was indeed and unmistakably gone. Having already lost patience over the uncertainty of the thing, this builder of houses for

157

the dead questioned no longer what was to be done. He immediately set himself to his supposed task.

That same night, as the minister was making plans to go to the farm, he passed Webster and his man in town, carrying the coffin through the darkness in the direction of Stonecross. He saw what it was, and his heart gave a throb of satisfaction. When the two men reached Stonecross in the pitch-blackness of a gathering storm, they stupidly set up their burden on end by the first door, then went to the other, where they made a vain effort to convey to the deaf Eppie a knowledge of what they had done. She made them no intelligible reply, so there they left the coffin, leaning up against the wall, and, eager to get back to their homes before the storm broke upon them, they set off at what speed was possible on the rough and dark road to Tiltowie, now in their turn passing the minister on his way.

By the time James arrived at the farm, it was too dark for him to see the ghastly sentinel standing at the nearest door. He walked into the parlor, and there met his father coming from the little room where his wife was seated.

To James's astonishment his father greeted him more cheerfully than usual. James cast a hurried, perplexed look on the face of the unburied dead, saw that it seemed in no way changed, and kept a bewildered silence.

"Isna this a most amazin' and hopeful thing?" cried his father. "What *can* there be to come oot o' it! Eh, but the ways o' the Almighty are truly no to be understood by mortal man! The lass must surely be intended for marvelous things to be dealt wi' after such an extra-ordnar' fashion! Night after night the bonny creature lies here, as quiet as if she had never seen trouble, for five days, and no change past upon her, no more than the three holy bairns in the fiery furnace! I'm jist in a tremble to think what's to come oot o' it all. God only kens! What do ye think, Jamie?—When the Lord was dead upon the cross, they waited but two nights, and there he was up and afore them! Here we hae waited these days—and naething even to prove that she's dead! still less any sign that she'll ever speak again!—What do ye think o' it, man?"

"If ever she returns to life, I greatly doobt she'll bring back her senses wi' her!'' said the mother, joining them from the inner chamber.

"I can think o' naething but that bonny lassie lyin' there neither dead nor alive! I jist wonder, James, that ye're no concerned and filled wi' doobt and even dread.''

"We're all in the hands of the God who created life and death,'' returned James in a pious tone.

The father held his peace.

"And he'll bring light oot o' the very dark o' the grave!'' said the mother.

Her faith, or at least her hope, once set going, went further than her husband's, and she had a greater power of waiting than he. James had sorely tried both her patience and her hope, and not even now had she given up on him.

"Ye'll bide and share oor watch this one night, Jamie?'' said Peter. "It's a ghostly kind o' thing to wake up in the dark wi' a dead corpse aside ye!—No that even yet I give her up for dead! but I canna help feelin' some eerie like—no to say afraid. Bide, man, and see the night oot wi' us.''

James had little inclination to add another to the party, and began to murmur something about his housekeeper. But his mother cut him short with an indignant remark.

"Hoot! what's a housekeeper aside o' kin?''

James had not a word to answer. Greatly as he shrank from the ordeal, he must encounter it without show of reluctance. He dared not even propose to sit in the kitchen instead. With better courage than will, he consented to share their vigil.

His mother went to prepare supper for them. His father rose, and saying he would have a look at the night, went toward the door; for nothing could quite smother the anxiety of the husbandman. But determined not to be left alone with that thing in the chamber, James glided past him and to the door.

In the meantime the wind had been rising, and the coffin had been tilting and resettling on its narrower end. When James opened the door, the gruesome thing fell forward just as he crossed the threshold, knocked him down, and fell over on top of him. His father, close behind, tumbled over the obstruction. "Curse the fule, Willie Webster!" he cried. "Had he naethin' better to do than send coffins aboot that naebody wanted—and then set them doon like rat traps to fall over poor Jamie!"

He lifted the thing off his son, who rose unhurt, but both amazed and offended at the mishap, and went back inside to join his mother in the kitchen.

"Dinna tell yer mither aboot the ill-fared thing, Jamie," said Peter, who then picked up the offensive vehicle, awkward burden as it was, and carried it to the back of the cornyard. There he shoved it over the low wall into the dry ditch at its foot, where he heaped dirty straw from the stable over it.

"It'll be long," he vowed to himself, "before Willie hears the last o' this!—and longer yet before he sees the glint o' the money he thought he was earnin' by it! the muckle idiot! He may turn it into a bread-kist, or whatever he likes, the gomf!"

Before he reentered the house, he walked a little way up the hill, to cast over the land a farmer's look of inquiry as to the coming night, and then went in, shaking his head at what the clouds boded.

Marion had brought their simple supper into the parlor, and was sitting there with James waiting for him. When they had ended their meal and Eppie had removed the remnants, the husband and wife went into the adjoining room and sat down by the bedside, where James presently joined them with a book in his hand. When she had cleaned up and *rested* the fire in the kitchen, Eppie came into the parlor and sat on the edge of a chair just inside the door.

Peter had said nothing about the night, and indeed, in his anger at the carpenter, had hardly paid much attention to how imminent the storm actually was. But the air had grown very sultry, and the night was black as pitch. It was plain that long before morning, a terrible storm must break. But midnight came and went, and all was very still.

Suddenly the storm broke upon them with a vibrating flash of angry lightning that seemed to sting their eyeballs, and was replaced the next instant by a darkness that seemed to crush them like a ponderous weight. Then all at once the weight itself seemed torn and shattered into sound—into heaps of bursting, roaring, tumultuous billows. Another flash, yet another and another followed, each with its crashing uproar of celestial avalanches.

At the first flash Peter had risen and gone to the large window of the parlor to discover, if possible, in what direction the storm was traveling. Marion followed him, and James was left alone with the dead. He sat, not daring to move. But when the third flash came, it flickered and played so long about the dead face that it seemed for minutes vividly visible, and his gaze remained fixed upon it, fascinated by what he saw.

The same moment, without a single preparatory movement, Isy was on her feet on top of the bed.

A great cry reached the ears of the father and mother. They hurried into the chamber. James lay motionless and senseless on the floor: a man's nerve is not necessarily proportioned to the hardness of his heart! The awful reality of the thing had overwhelmed him.

Isy had by now fallen, and lay gasping and sighing on the bed. She knew nothing of what had happened to her; she did not yet even know herself—and especially did not know that her faithless lover lay on the floor by her bedside.

When the mother entered, she saw nothing—only heard Isy's breathing. But when her husband came with a candle, and she saw her son on the floor, she forgot all about Isy. She dropped on her knees beside him and lamented over him as if he were dead.

But very different was the effect upon Peter when he saw Isy coming to herself. It was a miracle indeed! It could be nothing less! White as her face was, there was in it an unmistakable look of reviving life. When she opened her eyes and saw her master bending over her, she greeted him with a faint smile, closed her eyes again, and lay still. James soon also began to show signs of recovery, and his father turned to him.

With the old sullen look of his boyhood, he glanced up at his mother, still overwhelming him with caresses and tears.

"Let me up," he said in a complaining voice, wiping his face. "I feel so strange! What can have made me turn so sick all at once?"

"Isy's come to life again!" said his mother.

"Oh!" he returned.

"Ye're surely no sorry for that!" rejoined his mother, with a reaction of disappointment at his lack of sympathy. As she spoke she rose again to her feet.

"I'm pleased enough to hear it—why shouldn't I be?" he answered. "But she gave me a terrible start! You see, I never expected it as you did."

"Weel, ye *are* heartless!" exclaimed his father. "Hae ye nae spark o' fellow-feelin' wi' yer ain mither, when the lass comes to life that she's been mournin' these five days? But losh! she's off again—dead or in a dream, I kenna!—Is it possible she's aboot to slip frae oor hands again?"

James turned away and murmured something inaudible.

But Isy had only fainted, and after some eager ministrations on the part of Peter, she came to herself once more and lay breathing hard, her forehead wet as with the dew of death.

The farmer ran out to the loft in the yard, called the herd-boy, a clever lad, and told him to get up and ride for the doctor as fast as the mare could lay her feet to the road.

"Tell him Isy has come to life," he said, "and he must get oot here quick or she'll be dead again afore he gets to her. If ye canna get the one doctor, away wi' ye to the other, and dinna leave him till ye see him in the saddle and started. Then ye can ease up on the mare, and come home at yer leisure. He'll be here long afore ye! Tell him I'll pay him any fee he likes! Now away wi' ye like the very devil!"

When the boy returned on the mare's back a few minutes later, the farmer was waiting for him with a bottle of whiskey in his hand.

"Na, na!" he said, seeing the lad eye the bottle, "it's no for you! Ye need the small wit ye ever had. It's no *you* that has to gallop; ye hae but to stay on her back.—Here, Susy!"

He poured half a tumblerful into a soup-plate, then held it out to the mare who licked it up greedily, and immediately started off at a good pace.

Peter carried the bottle to the chamber and got Isy to swallow a little, after which she began to recover again. Nor did Marion forget to administer a share to James, who was not a little in need of it.

When the doctor arrived within an hour, full of amazed incredulity, he found Isy in a troubled sleep and James gone to bed.

23 / The Meeting

The next day, though very weak, Isy was much better. But she was too ill to get up, and Marion seemed now in her element, with two invalids to look after, both of whom were dear to her. She hardly knew for which to be more grateful—her son, given helpless into her hands, unable to repel the love she lavished upon him; or the girl whom God had taken from the very throat of the swallowing grave.

Her heart, at first bubbling over with gladness, eventually grew calmer when she came to realize how very ill James was, although she could not imagine the cause of his seeming collapse.

James was indeed not only very ill, but grew slowly worse, for he lay struggling at last in the Backbite of Conscience, who had him fixed in its hold and was giving him grave concern. From whence the holy dog came we know, but how he got hold of him to begin its saving torment, who can understand but God the maker of men. The beginnings of conscience, as all beginnings, are infinitesimal and wrapt in the mystery of creation.

I may venture to convey its results only, not its modes of operation or their stages. It was the wind blowing where it listed, doing everything and explaining nothing. The wind from the timeless and spaceless and formless region of God's feeling and God's thought blew open the eyes of this man's mind so that he saw and became aware that he saw. It blew away the long-gathered vapors of his self-satisfaction and conceit; it blew wide the windows of his soul that the sweet odor of his father's and mother's thoughts concerning him might enter. And when it entered he knew it for what it was; it blew back to him his own judgments of them and their doings, and he saw those judgments side by side with his new insights into their real thoughts and feelings. It blew away the desert of his own moral dullness, indifference, and selfishness that had so long hidden beneath them the watersprings of his own heart. It cleared all his conscious being and made him understand that he had never before loved his mother or his father, or anyone in fact; that he had never loved the Lord Christ, his Master, or cared in the least that he had died for him. He saw that he had never loved Isy—least of all when to himself he pleaded in his own excuse that he had loved her. That blowing wind, which he could not see nor could tell where it came from still less where it was going, began to blow together his soul and those of his parents.

For the first time the love in his father and in his mother drew him, and the memories of his childhood drew him, for the heart of God himself was drawing him. And as he yielded to that drawing, God continued to draw ever more and more strongly, until at last—I know not how God did it or what he did to the soul of James Blatherwick to make it different from what it was—but at last it grew capable of loving. First he yielded to his mother's love, because he could not help it; then he began to do something he had never done before in his life—he began to will to love others because he *could* love. With this start, he became conscious of the power to love and gradually grew to love still more. And thus did James at last start on the road toward becoming what he had to become or perish.

But before he reached this point, he had to pass through wild regions of torment and horror. He had to know himself all but mad. Both his body and soul had to be parched with fever, thirst, and fear. He had to sleep and dream lovely dreams of coolness and peace and courage, then wake and know that all his life he had been dead, and now first was coming to life. He saw for the first time that indeed it was good to be alive. He saw that now life was possible, because life was to love, and love was to live. What love was, or how he might lay hold of it, he still could not tell—he only knew that it came from and was the will and joy of the Father and the Son.

Even before his spiritual vision arrived at this point, the falseness and meanness of his behavior to Isy had become plain to him. The realization of what he had done brought with it such an overpowering self-contempt that he was tempted to destroy himself to escape the knowledge that he was himself the very man who had been such a creature who could do such things. But by and by he grew reconciled to the fact that he must live on; for otherwise, how could he do anything to make atonement for his actions? And with the thought of reparation, and with it possible forgiveness and reconcilement, his old love for Isy rushed in like a flood, at last grown into something more noble and more worthy of the word *love*. But until this final change arrived, his occasional bouts of remorse touched almost on madness, and for some time it seemed doubtful whether his mind might not retain a permanent tinge of insanity. During the time of his recovery, as he was ministered to by his mother, and his mental and spiritual journey, he came to feel a huge disgust for his position as parish minister. Occasionally he found himself bitterly blaming his parents for not interfering with his choice of a profession that had been his ruin and which he now detested.

One day he suddenly called out as they stood by his bed.

"Oh, Mother! oh, Father! *Why* did you allow me such hypocrisy? *Why* did you not bring me up as a farmer, to walk at the plough-tail? It was the pulpit that ruined me—the notion that I had to live up to the pattern of the minister even before recognizing anything real in myself! What a royal road to hypocrisy! Now I am lost. I shall never get back to bare honesty, not to say innocence! They are both gone forever!"

The poor mother could only imagine it his humility that made him accuse himself of hypocrisy because he had not fulfilled all the smallest details of his great office.

"Jamie, dear," she cried, "ye must cast yer care upon him that careth for ye! He kens ye hae done yer best, though not yer very best, for who could dare say that. Ye hae at least done what ye could!"

"Na, na," he answered, resuming the speech of his boyhood—a far better sign of him than his mother understood. "I ken too muckle, and that muckle too weel, to lay such flattering words to my sowl! It's jist as black as the night!"

"Hoots! ye're dreaming, laddie! The Lord kens his own. He'll see that they come through unburnt."

"The Lord doesna make any a hypocrite on purpose, doobtless. But if a man sin after he has once come to the knowledge o' the trowth, there remaineth for him—ye ken the rest o' it as weel as I do mysel', Mither! My only hope lies in the doobt o' whether I *had* ever come to a knowledge o' the trowth—or hae yet!—Maybe no!"

"Laddie, ye're no in yer right mind! It's fearsome to listen to ye!"

"It'll be worse to hear me roarin' wi' the rich man in the flames o' hell!"

"Peter! Peter!" cried Marion, driven almost to distraction, "here's yer own son, poor fellow, blasphemin' like one o' the condemned! He jist makes me shiver!"

But she received no answer, for at the moment her husband was nowhere near. In her despair she called out, "Isy! Isy! come and see if ye can do anything to quiet this sick bairn."

It was the third day of his fever, and by this time Isy was much better—able to eat and go about the house. She sprang from her bed, where at the moment she lay resting.

"Coming, mistress!" she answered.

She and James had not met since her resurrection, as Peter always called it.

"Isy! Isy!" cried James the moment he heard her approaching, "come in and hold the devil off me!"

He had risen to his elbow and was looking eagerly toward the door.

Isy entered. James threw his arms wide open, and with glowing eyes clasped her to him. She made no resistance. His mother would think it was all because of his fever. He immediately broke into wild words of love, repentance, and devotion.

"Don't heed him a hair, mem' he's clean out of his head!" Isy said in a low voice, making no attempt to free herself from his embrace, but treating him like a delirious child. "There must be something about me, mem, that quiets him a bit. It's in the brain, you know; the feverish brain! We mustn't contradict him; he must have his own way for a while."

But such was James's behavior to Isy that it was impossible for the mother not to suspect at least that this must not be the first time they had met. And presently she began to think to herself, as she examined her memory, that she must have seen Isy someplace before she ever came to Stonecross. But she could recall nothing.

By and by her husband came in to have his dinner. She sent Eppie up to take Isy's place, with the message that she was to come down at once. Isy obeyed, entered the kitchen a few moments later, where she dropped trembling into the first chair she came to. The farmer, already seated at the table, looked up anxiously.

"Bairn," he said, "ye're so pale! Ye're no fit to be aboot! Ye must be cautious, or ye'll be over the burn yet before ye're safe upon this side o' it! Preserve us all! We canna lose ye twice in one month!"

"Jist answer me one question, Isy, and I'll ask ye nae mair," said Marion.

"Na, na, never a question!" interrupted Peter; "no afore the shadow o' death has left the hoose! Draw ye up to the table, my bonny bairn."

But still Isy sat motionless, looking even more deathlike than while in her trance. Peter got up and made her swallow a little whiskey. When she revived, glad to put herself under his protection, she took the chair he had placed for her beside him, and made a futile attempt at eating.

"It's small wonder the poor thing hasna muckle appetite," remarked Mrs. Blatherwick, "considerin' the way yon ravin' laddie up the stairs has been carryin' on to her!"

"What's that?" asked her husband.

"But ye're no to make anythin' o' that, Isy!" added her mistress.

"Not a bit, mem," returned Isy. "I know well it means nothing but the heat of the burning brain! I'm right glad, though, that the sight of me did seem to comfort him some."

"Weel, I'm no sae sure!" answered Marion. "But we'll say nae more aboot that noo. My husband says no; and his word's law in this hoose."

Isy resumed her pretence of dining. Presently Eppie came down, went to her master, and said, "Andrew's come, sir, to ask after the yoong minister and Isy. Am I to ask him in?"

"Ay, and give him some dinner," answered the farmer.

The old woman set a chair for her son by the door, and proceeded to attend to him. James was thus left alone upstairs.

Silence again fell, and the appearance of eating was resumed, Peter and Andrew being the only ones who made a reality of it. Marion was occupied in her mind with many things, especially a growing doubt about Isy. The girl must have some secret, something having to do with their James. She had known something all the time; had she been taking advantage of their lack of suspicions? Thus she sat thinking and glooming.

All at once a cry of misery came from the room above. Isy started to her feet. But Marion was up before her.

"Sit doon this minute," she said in a commanding voice. "I'll gae to him mysel'!" And with the words she left the room.

Peter laid down his knife and fork, then half rose, staring bewildered by his wife's sharp speech, and finally followed her from the room.

"Oh, my baby! my baby!" cried Isy. "If only I still had you. It was God who gave you to me, or how could I love you so? And the mistress winna believe that I even had a bairnie! Noo she'll be sayin' that I killed my bonny wee man! And yet, even for *his* sake, I never once wished ye hadna been born! And noo, when the father o' him's ill, and cryin' oot for me, they winna let me near him!"

The last words left her lips in a wailing shriek.

Then first she saw that her master had reentered. Wiping her eyes hurriedly, she turned to him with a pitiful, apologetic smile.

"Dinna be sore angered wi' me, sir. I canna help bein' glad that I had him, though to lose him has given me such a sore heart."

Suddenly she stopped, terrified: how much had he heard? She did not even know what she might have said. But the farmer resumed his dinner and went on eating as if she had not spoken at all. But he had heard well enough nearly everything she said, and now sat inwardly digesting her words.

Isy was silent, saying to herself, "If only he loved me, I should be content and want nothing more. I would never even care if he said it. I would be so good to him that he could not help loving me a little!"

I wonder whether she would have been so hopeful had she known how his own mother had loved him, and how long she had looked in vain for any love from him in return. And when Isy vowed in her heart never to let James know that she had borne him a son, she never saw that in so doing she would be withholding from him the most potent of influences for his repentance and restoration to God and his parents.

She did not see James again that night. And before she fell asleep at last in the small hours of the morning, she had made up her mind that before the dawn had fully broken upon the moor, she would—as the best and only thing left her to do for him—be as far away from Stonecross as she could get.

She would go back to Deemouth, and again seek work in the paper mills.

24 / The Reunion

Isy awoke with the first of the gray dawn. The house was utterly still. She rose and dressed herself in soundless haste.

It was hard to leave, knowing James was still ill, but she had no choice. She held her breath and listened, but all was still. She opened her door softly; not a sound reached her ear as she crept down the stair. She did not have to unlock nor unbolt the door to leave the house, for it was never locked up.

A dreadful sense of the old wandering desolation came back upon her as she stepped across the threshold, and now she had no baby to comfort her! She was leaving a moldy peace and a withered love behind her, and had once more to encounter the rough, coarse world. It was with sadness that she left the place where she had found welcome, and where she had been loved, and where she had learned so much. She feared the moor she had to cross and the old dreams she must there encounter. But even in the midst of her loneliness in the growing light of dawn, she suddenly remembered that she had not left God, and that her Maker was with her and would not forsake her. In that knowledge she walked on, although she soon became very tired.

Of the several roads that led from the farm, the only one she knew was the one by which Mr. Robertson had first brought her to Stone-cross. She would take it back to the village where they had left the coach, and surely there she would be able to find some way to return to Aberdeen.

The walk was very tiring, for she was weak from her prolonged inactivity as well as from the crowd of emotions that had accompanied her recovery. Long before she reached Tiltowie, she was all but worn out. She stopped at the only house she had come to on the way and asked for a drink of water. The woman, the only person she had seen, for it was still early morning and the road was a rather deserted one, gave her milk instead. It strengthened her sufficiently for her to reach the end of her first day's journey; and for many days thereafter she did not have to make a second.

Isy had seen the cobbler once at the farm. And going about her work she had heard scraps of his conversations with the mistress. She had been greatly struck by certain of the things he said, and had often wished for the opportunity of a talk with him. As she reached the village on that same morning, walking along a narrow lane and hearing a cobbler's hammer at work, she glanced through a window of the house she was passing and at once recognized the soutar, John MacLear. He looked up as she obscured his light, and could scarcely believe his eyes to see before so early in the day Mrs. James Blatherwick's maid, concerning whom there had been such a marveling talk for days. She did not look well, and he wondered what she was doing up and so far from home.

She smiled to him and passed from the window with a respectful nod. He sprang to his feet, ran to the door, and overtook her at once.

"I'm jist aboot to drop my work, mem, and hae my breakfast. Will ye no come in and share wi' an auld man and a young lass? Ye hae come a right long way and look some tired."

"Thank you kindly, sir," returned Isy. "I *am* a bit tired! But how did you know who I was?"

"Weel, I canna jist say I ken ye by the name fowk call ye, and still less do I ken ye by the name the Lord calls ye. But none o' that matters so much to her that knows *he* has a name growin' for her—or rather, a name she's growin' to. Eh, what a day that will be when every habitant o' the holy city will walk the streets well kenned and weel kennin'!"

"Ay, sir, I understand you. For I heard you once say something like that to the mistress, the night you brought home the master's shoes to Stonecross. And I'm right glad to see you again."

They were already in the house, for she had followed him almost mechanically. The soutar was setting for her the only chair there was in the room when the cry of a child reached their ears.

The girl started to her feet. A rosy flush of delight overspread her countenance. She began to tremble from head to foot, and seemed almost on the point of either running toward the cry or fainting on the floor.

"Ay," exclaimed the soutar, with one of his sudden flashes of unquestioning insight, "by the look o' ye, ye ken that for the cry o' yer ain bairn, my bonny lass! Ye'll hae ben missin' him sorely, I don't doobt!—There! sit ye doon and I'll hae him in yer arms afore anither minute's past!"

She obeyed him and sat down, her eyes fixed wildly on the door. The soutar made haste and ran to fetch the child. When he returned with him in his arms, he found her sitting bolt upright with her hands already apart to receive him, and her eyes alive as he had never seen them before.

"My Jamie! My own bairn!" she cried, seizing him and drawing him to her with a grasp that, trembling, yet seemed to cling to him desperately, and a look almost of defiance, as if she dared the world to take him from her again.

"Oh, my God!" she cried in an agony of thankfulness. "I know you now! I know you now! Never more will I doubt you, my God!—Lost and found!—Lost for a wee, and found again forever!"

Then she caught sight of Maggie, who had entered the room behind her father, and now stood staring at her motionless—with a look of gladness indeed, yet not entirely of gladness.

"I know," Isy broke out, "that you're grudging me looking at him so. It's true that it's you that's been mothering him since I lost my wits. It's true that I ran away and left him. But ever since, I have sought him with my tears! You mustn't bear me any ill-will—There!" she added, holding him out to Maggie, "I haven't even kissed him yet! But you will let me kiss him before you take him away again?—my own bairnie, whose very coming I had to be ashamed of! Oh my God! But he knows nothing about it, and won't for years to come! I thank God that I haven't had to shoo the birds and the beasts off his bonny wee body! It might have been, but for you, my bonny lass!—and for you, sir!" she went on, turning to the cobbler.

Maggie took the child from her arms, then held up his little face for his mother to kiss, until he began to whimper a little. Then Maggie sat down with him in her lap, and Isy stood absorbed, looking at him.

At last she said with a deep sigh, "And now I must be gone, and I don't know how I'm to go! I have found him and I must leave him, but I hope not for very long! Maybe you'll keep him yet a while—say for a week or more. He's been so long unused to a vagrant life that I doubt it would well agree with him. And I must be away back to Aberdeen if I can get anybody to give me a lift."

"Na, na, that'll never do," returned Maggie, beginning to cry. "My father'll be glad enough to keep him. Only we hae no right over him, and ye must have him again when ye will."

"But you see I have no place to take him to," said Isy.

All this time the soutar had been watching the two girls with a divine look in his black eyes and rugged face. Now at last he opened his mouth and spoke.

"Ye need no ither place but right here," he said. "Go inside the hoose wi' Maggie, my dear. Lay ye doon on her bed, and she'll lay the bairnie beside ye, and bring yer breakfast there to ye.—Leave them there together, Maggie, my doo," he went on with infinite tenderness, "and come and give me a hand as soon as ye hae brewed the tea and gotten a loaf o' white bread. I'll hae my porridge a bit later."

Maggie obeyed at once, and took Isy to the other end of the house, where the soutar had long ago given up his bed to her and the baby.

When all had their breakfast, she sat down in her old place beside her father, and for a long time they worked together without a word spoken.

"I don't think, Father," said Maggie at length, "that I hae been attendin' to ye properly! I'm afraid the bairnie's been makin' me forget."

"No a hair, dautie!" returned the old soutar. "The needs o' the little one stood far afore mine; he *had* to be seen to first. And noo that we hae the mither o' him, we'll get on famously! Isna she a fine creature, and right mitherlike wi' the bairn? That was all I was concerned aboot. We'll get her story frae her before long, and then we'll ken better hoo to help her on wi' her life. And there can be nae fear but, atween you and me, and the Almighty at the back o' us, we'll hae bread enough for the quaternion o' us!"

He laughed at the odd word as it fell from his mouth and the Acts of the Apostles. Maggie laughed too, and wiped her eyes.

Before long Maggie realized that she had never been so happy in her life. Not only did she not have to give up the baby she had grown to love almost as much as if it had been her own, she gained a sister as well. Isy told them as much as she could without breaking her resolve to keep secret a certain name. She wrote to Mr. Robertson, telling him where she was and that she had found her baby. He came with his wife to see her, and thus began a friendship between the soutar and him which Mr. Robertson always declared one of the most fortunate things that had ever befallen him.

"That soutar-body," he would say, "knows more about God and his kingdom, the heart of it and the ways of it, than any man I ever heard of—and so humble!—just like the son of God himself!"

Before many days passed, however, a great anxiety laid hold of the little household, for wee Jamie was taken so ill that the doctor had to be sent for. For some days the child had a high fever and looked pitifully white. When first the illness came upon him and he ceased being so active, no one could please him but the soutar himself, and he, discarding his work at once, gave himself up to the child's service. Before long, however, he required more skillful handling, and then no one would do but Maggie, to whom he had been more accustomed. Isy could get no share in the labor of love except when he was asleep.

But Maggie was always very careful over the feelings of the poor mother, and though the child had to be in her own arms when awake, she would always, the minute he was securely asleep, lay him softly upon Isy's lap.

Maggie soon got high above her initial twinges of jealousy that one of the happiest moments in her life was when first the child consented to leave her arms for those of his mother. And when he was once more able to scurry about, Isy took her part with Maggie in putting hand and needle to the lining of the more delicate of the soutar's shoes.

25 / The Repentance

There was great concern, and not a little alarm at Stonecross because of the disappearance of Isy. But James continued so ill that his parents were hardly able to take much thought about anybody else.

At last the fever left him, and he began to recover, but he lay still and silent, seeming to take no interest in anything, and remembering nothing he had said. He hardly even remembered that he had seen Isy. And all the while his parents did not stop to wonder what could have caused such a sudden and inexplicable illness.

His weakened conscience was still at work in him, and had more to do with his feeble condition than the prolonged fever. At length his parents began to question his slow recovery and became convinced that he had something on his mind that was interfering with it. Both of them, in their own way, were confident it had to do with Isy. But whereas Marion had grown suspicious of the girl, her husband, having overheard certain of the words that fell from Isy when she thought herself alone, was intently though quietly waiting for what must follow.

"I don't doobt, Peter," began Marion one morning, after a long talk with the cottar's wife, who had been telling her of Isy's having taken up temporary lodgings with the soutar, "that the girl Isy had more to do wi' Jamie's attack than we ken. It seems to me he's long been broodin' over something we ken naethin' aboot."

"That would hardly be strange. When was it that we ever kent onything gaein' on in that mysterious laddie? Na, but he needs a good conscience of his own, for did anybody ever ken enough aboot it or him to say right or wrong to him? But if ye hae a thought he's ever wronged that lassie, I'll say he'll never come to health o' body or mind till he's confessed, and God has forgiven him. He *must* confess!"

"Hoot, Peter, dinna be sae suspicious o' yer own son. It's no like

177

ye. I wouldna let one ill thought o' poor Jamie inside this auld head o' mine! It's the lassie, I'll take my oath; it's that Isy that's at the bottom o' whate'er it is."

"Ye're too ready wi' yer oath, Marion, to what ye ken naethin' aboot! I say again, if he's done any wrong to that bonny creature—and it wouldna take ower muckle to convince me o' it—he'll hae to take his stand, minister or no minister, upon his repentance."

"Dare ye speak that way aboot yer ain son—ay, and mine, Peter Blatherwick! And the Lord's ordained minister besides!" cried Marion, driven almost to her wits' ends, but more by the persistent haunting of her own suspicion, which she could not repress, than the terror of her husband's words. "Besides," she added, "dinna ye see that nae doobt *he* wouldna be the first to fall into the snare o' a designin' woman, and would it be for his ain father to expose him to public contempt? Your part should be to cover up whatever little sin he may be wreslin' wi'."

"Dare *ye* speak o' a thing like that as a little sin? Do ye call lyin' and hypocrisy a little sin? I allow the sin itsel' may not be damnable alone, but hoo big might it not grow wi' other and worse sins upon the back o' it? Startin' wi' lyin' and little sins, a man may in the end grow to be a creature not fit to be pulled up wi' the weeds. Eh me, but my pride in the laddie! It'll be small pride for me if this fearsome thing turn oot to be true!"

"What could be such a fearsome thing? He's done nae ill thing, I tell ye."

Peter remained silent.

"And who would dare say it's true?" added Marion, almost fiercely.

"Nae one but himself. And if it be sae, and he doesna confess, the rod laid upon him'll be the rod o' iron that smashes a man like a crock o' clay.—I must take Jamie to task."

"Noo jist take ye care, Peter, that ye dinna quench the smokin' flax."

"I'm more likely to get the bruised reed into my naked palm," returned Peter. "But I'll say naethin, till he's a wee better, for we mustna drive him to despair!—Eh, if he would only repent! What I wouldna do to clear him—that is, to ken him innocent o' any wrong. I would die o' thanksgiving!"

"Well, we're nae called upon sae far as that," said Marion. "A lass is aye able to take care o' hersel'."

"God hae mercy upon the two o' them!" said Peter, and after that both parents were silent.

In the afternoon James was a good deal better, and when his father went in to see him, his first words were—"I doubt, Father, that I'm likely to preach again. I've come to see that I was never fit for the work, or had any call to it."

"It may be sae, Jamie," answered his father. "But we'll keep frae conclusions till ye're better and able to judge wi'oot the bias o' illness or distemper."

"But, Father," James went on, and for the first time since he was the merest child, Peter saw tears running down his cheeks. "I have been a terrible hypocrite! But my eyes are open at last. I see myself as I am."

"Weel, there's the Lord close by to take ye by the hand like Enoch. Tell me, laddie, hae ye anythin' on yer mind that ye would like to confess and be eased o' the burden frae it?"

James lay still for a few moments; then he said, almost inaudibly, "I think I could tell my mother better than you, Father."

"It'll all be one which one o' us ye tell. The forgivin' and the forgettin' will be one deed—by the two o' us at once! I'll go and cry doon the stair to yer mither to come up and hear ye." For Peter knew by experience that good notions must be taken advantage of in their first ripeness. "We mustna try the Spirit wi' any delays!" he added, as he went to the head of the stair, where he called aloud to his wife. Then returning to the bedside he resumed his seat, saying, "I'll jist bide a minute till she comes."

He did not want to let in any risk between his going and her coming, for he knew how quickly minds may change. But the moment she appeared, he left the room, gently closing the door behind him.

Then the trembling, convicted soul plucked up what courage his so long stubborn and yet cringing heart was capable of, and began.

"Mother, there was a lass I came to know in Edinburgh, when I was a divinity student there, and—"

"Ay, ay, I ken all aboot it!" interrupted his mother, eager to spare him; "—an ill-fared, designin' limmer that might hae kent better than to make advances to the son o' a respectable woman that way!—such, I doubtna, as would deceive the very elect!"

"No, no, Mother. She was none of that sort. She was both bonny and good, and pleasant to the heart as to the sight. She would have saved me if I had been true to her. She was one of the Lord's making, as he has made but a few."

"What for didna she keep away frae ye until ye had married her then? Dinna tell me she didna lay hersel' oot to make a prey o' ye?"

"Mother, you're slandering yourself!—I'll say not a word more."

"I'm sure neither yer father nor myself would hae stood in yer way frae marryin' her!" said Marion, retreating from the false position she had taken.

She did not know herself, or how bitter would have been her opposition to a marriage with one like Isy; for she had set her mind on a distinguished match for her Jamie.

"God knows how I wished I had kept a hold on myself! Then I might have stepped out of the dirt of my hypocrisy instead of falling head over heels into it. I was aye a hypocrite, but she would maybe have found me out and made me look at myself."

He did not know the probability that, if he had not fallen, he would have but sunk all the deeper in the worst bog of all, self-satisfaction, and nonetheless have played her false, and left her with a broken heart.

If anyone would argue that it would thus be better to do wrong and repent than to resist the devil in the first place, I warn him that in such a case he will not repent until the sorrows of death and the pains of hell itself lay hold upon him. An overtaking fault may be beaten out with a few stripes on the back. But a willful wrong shall not come out but by many stripes and a far deeper repentance. The doer of the latter must share, not with Judas, for he did repent, although too late, but with such as have taken from themselves the power of repentance.

"Was there no mark left o' her disgrace?" asked his mother, at last admitting to the dread possibility in full of what her son had done. "Wasna there a bairn to make it manifest?"

"None I ever heard tell of."

"In that case, she's no muckle the worse, and ye needna go on lamentin'," said Marion, the justifying spirit now full at work in her. *"She'll* no be the one to tell! And *ye* mustna, for her sake! Sae take comfort over what's gone and done wi, and canna come back again, and mustna happen again.—Eh, but it's God mercy there was nae bairn!"

Thus had the mother herself become an evil counselor, crying, "Peace! peace!" when there was no peace, and tempting her son to continue on in his falsehood and become a devil. But one thing yet rose up for the truth in his miserable heart—his reviving and growing love for Isy. It had seemed smothered in selfishness, but was alive and operative, God only knows how—perhaps through feverish, incoherent, forgotten dreams.

He had expected his mother to help him in his repentance, even should the path before him be one of social disgrace. He knew that repentance and reparation must go hand in hand. He had been the cowering slave of a false reputation, but his illness had roused him, set repentance before him, brought confession within sight, and purity within the reach of prayer. But he was surprised at her resistance in his attempt to do what he now knew to be right.

"I must go to her," he cried, "the minute I'm able to be up!—Where is she, Mother?"

"Upon nae account see her, Jamie! It would be but to fall again into her snare!" answered his mother, with decision in her look and tone. "We're to abstain frae all appearance o' evil—as ye ken better than I can tell ye."

"But Isy's not an appearance of evil, Mother."

"Ye say weel there, I confess. Na, she's no an appearance; she's the very thing! Keep frae her, as ye would frae the ill one himsel'!"

"Did she ever let on what there had been between us?"

"Na, never. She kenned well what would come o' that!"

"What, Mother?"

"The ootside o' the door!"

"Do you think she told anybody?"

"Many a one, I don't doobt."

"Well, I don't believe it. I am sure she's been as silent as death."

"Hoo ken ye that?—Why didna she say a word to yer ain mither?"

"Because she was set on holding her tongue. Was she to bring such a tale of me to the very house I was born in? As long as I hold my tongue, she'll never wag hers.—Eh, but she's a true one! *She's* one you can trust!"

"Weel, I allow she's done as a woman should—the fault bein' her ain."

"The fault being mine, Mother; she wouldn't tell what would disgrace me."

"She might hae kenned her secret would be safe wi' me."

"I might have said the same but for the way you are speaking of her this very minute! Where is she, Mother? Where's Isy?"

"'Deed, she's made a moonlight flight o' it."

"I told you she would never tell on me! Did she have any money?"

"Hoo can *I* tell?"

"Did you pay her any wages?"

"She gae me no time! But she's no likely to tell noo, for hearin' her tale, who would take her in?"

"Eh, Mother, but you are hardhearted."

"I ken a harder, Jamie!"

"That's me! And you're right, Mother! But if you would have me love you from this minute to the end of my days, be a little fair to Isy. I have been a damned scoundrel to her!"

"Jamie, Jamie! Ye're provokin' the Lord to anger—swearin' like that in his very face—and you a minister."

"'Tis hardly swearing, Mother, when I speak only the truth. I provoked him a heap worse when I left Isy to suffer her shame. Don't you remember how the Apostle Peter cursed when he said to Simon, 'Go to hell with your money'?"

"She's told the soutar anyway."

"What! Has *he* gotten a hold of her?"

"Ay, he has! And dinna ye think it'll be all over the toon long afore this?"

"And how will you face the truth, Mother?"

"We must tell yer father and get him to quiet the soutar! For *her*, we must jist stop her mouth with a bunch o' bank notes.''

"That would make it almost impossible for even her to forgive you or me either any longer.''

"And who's she to speak o' forgivin'?''

The door opened and Peter entered. He strode up to his wife and stood over her like an angel of vengeance. His very lips were white with wrath.

"After thirty years o' married life, noo first to ken my wife as a messenger o' Satan!'' he panted.

She fell on her knees before him.

"But think o' Jamie, Peter!'' she pleaded. "I would lose my sowl for Jamie.''

"Ay, and lose his as weel!'' he returned. "Lose what's yer own to lose—and that's no yer sowl, nor yet Jamie's! He's no yours to save, but ye're doing all ye can to destroy him—and perhaps ye'll succeed! Would ye send him straight away to hell for the sake o' a good name—a lie! a hypocrisy! Call ye that bein' a Christian mither, Marion?—But, Jamie, I'm off to the toon, on me two feet, for the mare's crippled—the very de'il's in the hoose and the stable and all it would seem! I'm away to fetch Isy home! And, Jamie, ye'll jist tell her afore me and yer mither that as soon as ye're able to crawl to the kirk wi' her, ye'll marry her afore the world and take her home to the manse wi' ye.''

"Hoot, Peter! Would ye disgrace him afore all the beggars o' Tiltowie?''

"Ay, and afore God, that kens all things wi'oot anybody tellin' him! My hand and heart shall be clear o' this abomination!''

"Marry a maiden that never said na?—a lass that's nae a maiden, nor ever will be!—Hoots!''

"And who's to blame for that?''

"She is hersel'!''

"Na, Marion, 'tis Jamie and nae other! I'm surprised at ye! Oot o' my sight I tell ye! Lord, I kenna hoo I'm to win over this!''

He turned from her with a groan and went toward the open door, almost like one struck blind.

"Oh, Father!'' cried James, "forgive my mother before you go or my heart will break. It's the awfulest thing to see the two of you arguing this way.''

"She's no sorry one bit for what she's said,'' replied Peter.

"I am, I am, Peter!'' cried Marion, breaking down at once. "Do what ye will, and I'll follow ye—only let it be done quietly, wi'oot din or proclamation. Why should everybody ken everythin'? Who has the right to see into other folk's hearts and lives? The world could hardly go on if that was the way o' it.''

"Father,'' said James, "I thank God that now you know all. Such a weight it takes off me! I'll be well now in no time! I think I'll go to Isy myself. But I wish you hadn't come in quite so soon. For I wasn't giving in to my mother. I was but thinking how to say what was in me to say without making her more upset than could be helped. Believe me, Father, if you can, that I was determined to confess all, no matter what she may have said to me.''

"I believe ye, my bairn, and I thank God I hae that muckle power o' belief left in me. I confess I was in too great a hurry, and I'm sure ye were takin' the right way wi' yer poor mither. Ye see, she loved ye sae weel that she could think o' naething or naebody but yersel'. That's the way wi' mithers, Jamie, if ye only kenned it! She was close to sinnin' an awful sin for yer sake, man!''

He turned again to his wife.

"That's what comes o' lovin' the praise o' men, Marion. Easy it passes into the fear o' men and disregard o' the Holy.—But I'm away down to the soutar, and tell him the change that's come over us. He'll nae doobt be a hair surprised!''

"I'm ready to go with you, Father—or will be in a minute!'' said James, getting ready to spring out of bed.

"Na, na; ye're no fit!'' interposed his father. "I would hae to be takin' ye on my back afore we was at the foot o' the brae! Stay at home and keep yer mither company.''

"Ay, bide, Jamie, and I winna come near ye,'' sobbed his mother.

"Anything to please you, Mother—but I'm more fit than my father thinks,'' said James as he settled down again in bed.

So Peter went, leaving mother and son silent together.

At last the mother spoke.

"It's the shame o' it, Jamie,'' she said.

"The shame was in what I did, Mother, and in hiding from that shame," he answered. "Now I have but the dregs to drink, and them I must endure with patience, for I have well deserved to drink them! But poor Isy, she must have sorely suffered! I hardly dare think what she must have come through."

"Her mither couldna hae brought her up right. The first o' the fault lay in the upbringin'."

"There's another whose upbringing wasn't to blame. *My* upbringing was all it ought to have been—and see how bad I turned out!"

"It wasna what it ought to hae been. I see it all plain noo! I was aye too afraid o' makin' ye hate me, and sae I didna train ye like I should.—Oh, Isy, Isy, I hae done ye wrong. I ken ye could never hae laid yersel' oot to snare him—it wasna in ye to do it."

"Thank you, Mother! It was truly all my fault. And now my life shall go to make it up to her."

"And I must see to the manse," rejoined his mother, "to put all in order for ye."

"As you like, Mother. But for the manse, I will have to clear out of that. I can speak no more from that pulpit! I've been a hypocrite in it too long already. The thought of it makes me shudder!"

"Speak na like that o' the pulpit, Jamie, where so many holy men hae stood up and spoken the Word o' God. Ye'll be a burnin' and shinin' light in that pulpit before many a long day after we're dead and home."

"The more holy men that have there borne witness, the less dares any living lie stand there bragging and blazing in the face of God and man. It's shame of myself that makes me hate the place, Mother. Once and no more will I stand there, making of it my stool of repentance, and then down the steps and away, like Adam from the garden."

"And what's to come o' Eve? Are ye goin', like him, to say, 'The woman thou gavest to me—it was all her fault'?"

"You know I'm takin the blame upon myself."

"But hoo can ye take it upon yersel' if ye stand up there an' confess? Fowk'll aye give her a full share in the blame at least. Ye must hae some care o' the lass—that is, if after all ye're goin' to make her yer wife, as ye profess. And what are ye goin' to turn yer hand to next, seein' ye hae already laid it to the plough and turned back?"

"To the plough again, Mother—the real plough this time! From the kirk door I'll come home like the prodigal to my father's house and say to him, 'Set me to the plough, Father. See if I can't be something like a son to you after all'!"

26 / The Forgiveness

Thus wrought in young James Blatherwick—pastor, sinner, and soon to be child of God—that mighty power, mysterious in his origin as marvelous in its result, which had been at work in him all the time he lay sick and overwhelmed with feverish phantasms. But the result was certainly no phantasm. His repentance was true. He had been dead, and was alive again! God and the man met at last! As to *how* God turned the man's heart, that shall remain the eternal mystery. We can only say, "Thou, God, knowest." To understand that we should have to go down below the foundation of the universe itself, underneath creation, and there see God send out from himself man, the spirit, forever distinguished yet never divided from the Lord, forever dependent upon and growing in him, never complete outside of him because his origin, his very life is founded in the Infinite; never outside of God, because in him only he lives and moves and breathes and grows, and *has* his being.

Brothers and sisters, let us not linger to ask how these things can be. Let us turn at once to this Being in whom the *I* and *me* are created and have meaning, and let us make haste to obey him. Only in obeying shall we become all we are capable of being; thus only shall we learn and understand all we are capable of learning and understanding. The pure in heart shall see God; and to see him is to know all things.

Thoughts similar to these were in the meditations of the soutar as he watched the farmer stride away into the dusk of the gathering twilight, going home with a light heart to his wife and repentant son. Peter had told the cobbler that James's sickness had brought to light a sin of his youth whose concealment had been long troubling him, and that he was now bent on making all the reparation he could.

"Mr. Robertson," said Peter, "brought the lass to oor hoose, never sayin' a word aboot Jamie, for he didna ken they were anythin' to one anither. And the girl never said one word aboot him to us."

The soutar went to the door and called Isy. She came, and stood humbly before her old master.

"Weel, Isy," said the farmer kindly, "ye gave us a clever slip yon mornin', and a bit of a fright besides! What possessed ye to do such a thing, lass?"

She stood, in obvious distress, and made no answer.

"Hoot, lassie, tell me," insisted Peter. "I haena been an ill master to ye, have I?"

"Sir, you have been like the master of us all to me. But I can't— that is, I mustn't—or rather, I'm determined not to say a word of the thing to anybody."

"Did ye think my wife was afraid the minister might fall in love wi' ye?"

"Well, sir, there might have been something like that in it. But I so wanted to find my bairn again, for in that trance I lay so long, I saw or heard something I took for a sign that he was still alive, and not that far away.—And—would you believe it, sir?—in this very house I found him, and here I have him, and I'm just as happy now as I was miserable before. Is it wrong of me that I can't be sorry anymore?"

"And noo," said Mr. Blatherwick, "ye hae but one thing left to confess—and that's who's the father o' him."

"No, that I can't do, sir. It's enough that I've disgraced *myself*! You wouldn't have me disgrace another as well! What good would that be?"

"It would help ye bear the disgrace."

"No, not a hair, sir. *He* couldn't stand the disgrace half so well as me. I reckon the man's the weaker vessel; the woman has her bairn to fend for, and that takes her thoughts off the shame."

"Ye dinna tell me he gives ye naethin' to help ye maintain the child?"

"I tell you nothing, sir. He never even knew there was a child!"

"Hoot, toot! ye canna be sae simple. It's no possible ye never told him and that he didna ken!"

"I was too 'ashamed. Ye see, it was all my fault—and it was naebody's business. I wasn't going to have *his* name mixed up with a lass like myself. So I went away, and he never saw me again, and he never heard nothing of the child. And you mustn't try to make me tell you, for I have no right to, and surely you can't have the heart to make me!—But that you shall not anyway! For I won't tell!''

"I dinna blame ye, Isy. But there's jist one thing I'm determined aboot—and that is that the rascal shall marry ye.''

Isy's face flushed. She had been taken too much by surprise to hide her pleasure at such a thought. But the flush faded, and presently Mr. Blatherwick saw that she was fighting within herself. Then the shadow of a crafty smile flitted across her face.

"Surely you wouldn't marry me to a rascal, sir," she answered. "Ill as I behaved to you, I can hardly have deserved that at your hand.''

"That's what he'll hae to do, though—jist marry ye! I'll make him!''

"I won't have him forced! It's me that has the right over him, and no other man or woman. He shall not be made to act against his will. What would you have me—thinking I would take a man that was forced to marry me. No, no, there can't be none of that! And you can't make *him* marry me if *I* won't marry him!—No, thank you.''

"Weel, my bonny lady," said Peter, "ye're some yoong lassie. If I had a prince for a son, I would tell ye that ye could hae him— provided he was worth the takin'.''

"And I would say to you, sir, 'No—not if he wasn't willing,' '' answered Isy, and ran from the room.

"Weel, what do ye think o' the lass by this time, Mr. Blather-wick?'' said the soutar, with a flash in his eye.

"I think jist what I thought afore," answered Peter; "she's one in a million. If Jamie isna ready to leave father and mother and kirk and steeple, and cleave to that young woman and her only, he's no a mere fool, he's a miserable wicked fool, and I'll never speak a word to him again, wi' my will, if I live to the age o' auld Methuselah!''

"Take care what ye say to him, though—Isy'll be upon ye! Ye mustn't try to persuade him," said the soutar, laughing. "But listen to me, Mr. Blatherwick, and don't say a word to the minister aboot the bairnie.''

"Na, na. It'll be best to let him find that oot for himsel'.—And noo I must be gaein."

He strode to the door, holding his head high, and left without another word. The soutar closed the door and returned to his work, saying aloud as he went, "Lord, let me ever and aye see thy face and desire nothing more—except that the whole world, O Lord, may behold it likewise!"

Peter Blatherwick went home joyous at heart. His son was his son again—and no villain!—only a poor creature, as is every man until he turns to the Lord and leaves behind him every ambition and care for the judgment of men. He rejoiced that the girl he and Marion had befriended would be a strength to his son, that she had proved herself to be a right noble young woman. And he praised the Father of men that the very wanderings and backslidings of those he loved had brought about their repentance and restoration.

"Here I am!" he cried as he entered the house. "I hae seen the lass once more, and she's better and bonnier than ever!"

"Ow ay! Ye're jist like all the men I ever kenned," said Marion with a smile; "—easily taken in wi' the skin-side!"

"Doobtless! For the Maker has taken a heap o' pains wi' the skin! Anyway, yon lassie's a special one, I can tell ye that. Jamie should be on his knees to her this very moment—no sittin' there gazin' as if his two eyes were two bullets, fired off but never got oot o' their barrels!"

"Hoot, would ye hae him go on his knees to any but the one?"

"Ay, would I—to one that's nearer God's likeness than he has been to her—and that's oor Isy.—I think, Jamie, that ye might be fit for a drive in the mornin'. I'll take ye to the toon if ye be ready, and let ye say whate'er ye hae to say to her."

James agreed. He did not sleep much that night, yet nevertheless was greatly improved by the next day and well able to get out of bed. Before noon they were at the soutar's door. MacLear opened it himself and took the minister straight to the ben-end of the house, where Isy sat alone. She rose, and with downcast eyes went to meet him.

"Isy," he faltered, "can you forgive me? And will you marry me as soon as we're able? I'm ashamed of myself as I can be!"—

"You don't have so much to be ashamed of as I do. It was my fault."

"But to not hold my face to it! Isy, I have been a scoundrel to you! I'm so disgusted with myself I can hardly look myself in the face."

"You didn't know where I was! I ran away so nobody would know."

"What reason was there for anybody to know? I'm sure you never told."

Isy went to the door and called Maggie. James stared after her, bewildered.

"This was the reason," she said, reentering with the child and laying him in James's arms.

He gasped with astonishment.

"Is this mine?" he stammered.

"Yours and mine," she replied. "Wasn't God a heap better than I deserved? Such a bonny bairn! Not a mark, not a spot on him from head to foot to tell that he had no business to be here!—Give the bonny wee man a kiss. Hold him close to you, and he'll take the pain out of your heart. He's your own son! He came to me bringing the Lord's forgiveness long before I had the heart to ask for it. Eh, but we must do our best to make it up to God's bairn for the wrong we did him before he was born! But he'll be like his great Father, and forgive us both."

As soon as Maggie had given the child to his mother, she went to her father and sat down beside him, crying softly. He turned on his leather stool and looked at her.

"Rejoice wi' them, Maggie, my doo," he said. "Ye haena lost the one; ye hae gained the two! God himsel' is glad, and the Shepherd's glad, and the angels are all makin' such a flut-flutter wi' their muckle wings, that I can almost hear them!"

Maggie turned to him, wiped her eyes, and smiled. Thereafter her tears were ones of unrestrained joy.

I will not dwell on the delight of James and Isobel, thus restored to each other, the one from a sea of sadness, the other from a gulf of perdition. The one had deserved many stripes, the other but a few. Needful measure had been measured to each, and repentance had brought them together. Our sins and our iniquities shall be no more remembered against us when we take refuge with the Father of Jesus and of us. Nothing we have done can separate us from Him—nothing except our abiding in the darkness and refusing to come to the light.

Before James left the house, the soutar took him aside and said, "Dare I offer ye a word o' advice?"

"Indeed you may!" answered the young man with humility. "How would it be possible for me to keep from doing anything you might tell me; for you and my father and Isy between you have saved my very soul!"

"Weel, I would jist ask that ye take no further step o' consequence afore ye see Mister Robertson. Ye see, I would like to see ye put yersel's in the hands o' a man that kens ye both, and the half o' yer story already. Then take his advice what ye ought to do next."

"I will—and thank you, Mr. MacLear! One thing only I hope—that neither you nor he will seek to persuade me to go on preaching. One thing I'm set on, and that is to deliver my soul from hypocrisy, and to walk softly all the rest of my days. Happy man would I have been had they set me from the first to follow the plough and cut the grain and gather the stooks into the barn—instead of creeping into a leaky boat to fish for men with a foul and tangled net! I'm affronted and ashamed of myself!—Eh, the presumption of the thing! But I have been well and righteously punished! The Father drew his hand out of mine and let me try to go on alone. And down I came! For I was fit for nothing but to fall. Nothing less could have brought me to myself—and it took a long time. I hope Mr. Robertson will see the thing as I do myself."

The very next day Peter and James set out together for Aberdeen, and the news which father and son carried them filled the Robertsons with more than pleasure. And if their reception of him made James feel like the repentant prodigal he was, it was by its heartiness and their jubilation over Isy.

The next Sunday Mr. Robertson preached in James's pulpit, announcing the engagement between James Blatherwick and Isobel Rose. The two following Sundays he repeated his visit to Tiltowie, and on the third Monday married them at Stonecross. Then also was the little one baptized, by the name of Peter, in his father's arms—

amid much gladness, not unmingled with a humble and righteous shame. The soutar and Maggie were the only friends present besides the Robertsons.

Before the gathering broke up, the farmer put his big Bible into the hands of the soutar, with the request that he would lead their prayers. This was very nearly what he said:

"O God, to whom we belong heart and soul, body and blood and bones, hoo great thou art, and hoo close to us. You only, Lord, hold true ownership ower us! We bless thee heartily, rejoicin' in what thou hast made us, and still more in what thou art thysel'. Take to thy heart and hold them there, these thy two repentant sinners, and thy own little one and theirs, who's innocent as thou hast made him. Give them such grace to bring him up that he be none the worse for the wrong they did him afore he was born. And let the knowledge o' his parents' fault hold him safe frae anything suchlike in his own life. And may they both be the better for their fall, and live a heap more to the glory o' their Father because o' that slip! And if ever again the minister should preach thy Word, may it be wi' the better un'erstandin', and the more fervor. And to that end give him the height and depth and breadth and length o' thy forgivin' love. Thy name be glorified! Amen!"

"I'll never preach again!" whispered James to the soutar as they rose from their knees.

"I winna be altogether sure o' that!" returned the soutar. "Doobtless, ye'll do as the Spirit shows ye."

James made no answer. The next morning, James sent to the clerk of the synod his resignation of his parish and office.

No sooner had Marion, repentant under her husband's terrible rebuke, set herself to resist her rampant pride than the indwelling goodness swelled up in her like a reviving spring, and she began to be her old and lovely self again. Little Peter, whom they had renamed after his grandfather, with his beauty and winsome ways, melted and scattered the last lingering rack of her fog-like ambition for her son. Twenty times in a morning would she drop her work to catch up and caress her grandson, overwhelming him with endearments, while over the return of his mother, now her second daughter indeed, she was jubilant.

From the first announcement of the proposed marriage, she had begun cleaning and setting to rights the parlor, making it over entirely for Isy and James's use. But the moment Isy discovered her intent, she protested obstinately. The very morning after the wedding she was down in the kitchen, and had put the water on the fire for the porridge before her husband was awake. Before her new mother was down or her father-in-law came in from his last preparations for the harvest, it was already boiling, and the table laid for breakfast.

"I know well," she said to her mother, "that I have no right to counter you. But you were glad enough of my help when I first came to be your servant-lass, and why shouldn't things be just the same now? I know all the ways of the place and that they'll leave me plenty of time for the bairnie. You must just let me step again into my own old place. And if anybody comes, it won't take me a minute to make myself tidy as becomes a minister's wife.—Only he says that's to be all over now, and there'll be no need."

With that she broke into a little song, and went on with her work, singing.

At breakfast, James made a request of his father that he might turn a certain unused loft into a room for himself and Isy and little Peter. His father made no objection, and thus he set about the scheme at once, but was interrupted in his work by the speedy beginning of an exceptionally plentiful harvest.

The very day the cutting of the oats began, James appeared on the field with the other scythe-men, prepared to do his best. What delighted his father even more than his work—which began slowly as he learned the way, but soon made rapid progress—was the way he talked with the men and women in the field. Every show of superiority had vanished from his bearing and speech, and he was simply himself, behaving like the others, only with greater courtesy.

When the hour for the noonday meal arrived, Isy appeared with her mother-in-law and old Eppie, carrying the food for the laborers and leading little Peter in her hand. For a while the company was enlivened by the child's merriment, after which he was laid with his bottle in the shadow of an overarching stook of grain, and went to sleep, his mother watching him while she took her first lesson in gathering and binding the sheaves. When he awoke, his grandfather sent the whole family home for the rest of the day.

"Hoots, Isy, my dauty," he said when she protested that she could well finish her work, "would ye make a slave driver o' me, and bring disgrace upon the name o' yer father?"

Then she smiled and obeyed, and went at once with her husband, both of them tired indeed, but happier than they had ever before been in their lives.

27 / The Healing

The next morning James was in the field with the rest long before the sun was up. Day by day he grew stronger in mind and in body, until at length he was not only quite equal to the harvest work, but capable of anything required of a farm servant.

His deliverance from the slavery of Sunday prayers and sermons, and his consequent sense of freedom and its delight, greatly favored his growth in health and strength. Before the winter came, however, he had begun to find his heart turning toward the pulpit with a waking desire to again expound God's truths, this time with reality. For almost as soon as his day's work ceased to exhaust him, he had begun to take up the study of the sayings and doings of the Lord of men, eager to verify the relation in which he stood toward him, and through him, toward that eternal atmosphere in which he lived and moved and had his being, God himself.

One day, with a sudden questioning hunger, he rose in haste from his knees and turned almost trembling to his Greek New Testament, to find whether the words of the Master, "If any man will do the will of the Father," meant "If any man *is willing* to do the will of the Father." Finding that to be just exactly what they did mean, he was able to be at rest sufficiently to go on asking and hoping. And it was not long thereafter before he began to feel he had something worth telling, and must tell it to anyone that would hear. Heartily he set himself to pray for that spirit of truth, which the Lord had promised to them that asked it of their Father in heaven.

He talked with his wife about what he had found. Then he talked with his father and later the soutar.

The cobbler had for many years made a certain use of his Sundays by which he now saw he might be of service to James: He went four miles into the country to a farm on the other side of Stonecross to hold a Sunday school. It was the last farm for a long way in that direction. Beyond it lay an unproductive region, consisting mostly of peat moss and lone, barren hills—where the waters above the firmament were but imperfectly divided from the waters below the firmament. There roots of the hills came rather close together and the waters gathered, making many marshy places, with only very occasionally here and there a patch of ground on which crops could be raised.

There were, however, many more houses, such as they were, than could have been expected from the appearance of the district. In one spot, indeed, not far from this farm, there was even a small, thin hamlet. It was a long way from church or parish-school, so without anyone to minister to the spiritual needs of the people, it had become a rather rough and ignorant place, with a good many superstitions—none of them in their nature especially mischievous, except indeed as they blurred the idea of divine care and government. It was just the sort of place for bogill-baes and brownie-baes, boodies, goblins, and water-kelpies to linger and disport themselves, long after they had disappeared elsewhere.

Therefore, when the late minister came seeking his counsel, the cobbler proposed, without giving any special reason for it, that he should accompany him the next Sunday afternoon to his school at Bogiescratt. James consented, and the soutar called for him at Stonecross on his way.

"Mr. MacLear," said James as they walked along the rough parish road together, "I have but just arrived at a point I ought to have reached before I ever entertained a thought of addressing anyone about religion. Perhaps I knew some little things *about* religion, but certainly I knew nothing *of* it, least of all had I made any discoveries for myself in spiritual matters. And before that, how can a man possibly understand or know anything whatever about it? Even now I may be presuming to dare to say so, but at least I seem to have begun to recognize a little of the relation between a man and the God who made him. And with the sense of that, as I was saying to you last Friday, there has risen in my mind a new desire to communicate to my fellow-men something of what I have seen and learned. One thing I hope at least, that I shall henceforth be free from any temptation to show off or elevate myself above anyone, and I pray that at first hint of such I shall be immediately made aware of my danger and be given the grace to pull myself out of that pit. And one thing I have resolved upon—that if ever I preach again, I will never again *write* a sermon. I know I shall make many blunders, and do the thing very badly. But failure itself will keep me from conceit—will keep me, I hope, from thinking of myself at all, enabling me to leave myself in God's hands, and willing to fail if he please. Don't you think that we ought to be able to place ourselves as confidently in God's hands as did the early Christians?"

"I do that, Master James!" answered the soutar. "Hide yersel' in God, and when ye rise before men, speak oot o' that secret place— and fear naethin'. Look yer congregation straight in the eye and say what at the moment ye think and feel, and dinna hesitate to give them the best ye hae."

"Do you really think the Lord might be able to use me again? I mean to speak to his people?"

"Who can tell? We must wait on his guidance. But to answer yer question—ay, do I think he can! If he pleases, which I hope he will!"

"Thank you, thank you, sir! I think I understand," replied James. "If ever I do speak again, I should like it to begin in your school."

"Ye shall then—this very day, if ye like, if ye feel the Lord callin' ye to do so," rejoined the soutar. "I think ye hae somethin', even noo, upon yer mind that ye would like to say to them—but we'll see hoo ye feel aboot it after I hae said a word to them first."

"When you have said what you want to say, Mr. MacLear, give me a look. If I have anything to say, I will respond to your sign. Then you can introduce me, saying what you will."

The cobbler held out his hand to his new disciple, and they continued their journey mostly in silence.

When they reached the farmhouse, the small gathering was nearly complete. It was comprised mostly of farm laborers, but a few of the group worked in a quarry, where serpentine lay under the peat. In this serpentine there occasionally occurred veins of soapstone, of such thickness as to be itself the object of the quarrier. It was used in the making of porcelain, and small quantities were needed for other purposes.

When the soutar began, James was a little shocked at first to hear him use his mother-tongue as if in ordinary conversation. He put on no preachy tone or airs, and it was completely different from anything James had ever heard from any pulpit. But any sense of its unsuitableness soon vanished, and James began to feel that the vernacular gave his friend additional power of expression.

"My frien's," he began, "I was jist thinkin' as I came ower the hill, hoo we were all made wi' different powers—some o' us able to do one thing best, and some anither. And that led me to remark that it was the same wi' the world we live in—some parts o' it fit for growin' oats, and some barley, and some wheat, or potatoes, and hoo every varyin' piece has to be turned to its own best use. We all ken what a lot o' uses the bonny green-and-red mottlet marble can be put to. But it wouldna do weel for buildin' hooses, specially if there were many streaks o' soapstone in it. Still it's not that the soapstone itsel's o' na use, for ye ken there a heap o' uses it can be put to. For one thing, the tailor takes a bait o' it to mark where he's to send the shears along the cloth when he's cuttin' oot a pair o' breeches. And again they mix it up wi' the clay they take for the finer kind o' crockery. But upon the ither hand, there's one thing it's used for by some that canna be considert a right use to make o' it. There's one wild tribe in America they tell me that eat a heap o' it—and that's a thing I canna un'erstan.

"But ye see what I'm drivin' at? It's this—that things hae aye to be put to their right uses. There are good uses, and there are better uses, and then there are aye the *best* uses. And where a thing can be put to its best use, it's a shame to put them to any ither use but that.

"Noo, what's the best use o' a man—what's a man made for? The catechism says, *to glorify God.* And hoo is he to do that? Jist by doin' the will o' God. For the one perfect man said he was born into the world for that one special purpose—to do the will o' him that sent him. A man's for a heap o' uses, but that one use covers them all. When he's doin' the will o' God, he's doin' all things. Still there are various ways in which a man can be doin' the will o' his Father in heaven, and the great thing for each one is to find oot the best way *he* can set aboot doin' that will.

"Noo, here's a man sittin' aside me that I must help set to the best use he's fit for—and that is, telling ither fowk what he kens aboot the God that made him and them, and stirrin' them up to do what the Lord would hae them do. The fact is, that the young man was once a minister o' the Kirk o' Scotland, but when he was a yoong man, he fell into a great fault—a yoong man's fault—I'm no gaein to excuse it—dinna think that. Only I charge ye to remember hoo many things ye hae done yersel's that ye hae to be ashamed o', though some o' them may never come to the light. And be sure o' this—my friend has repented right sorely. Like the prodigal, he grew ashamed o' what he had done, and he gave up his kirk and went home to work on his father's farm. And that's what he's at noo, even though he be a scholar, and a right good one. And by his repentance, he's learnt a heap that he didna ken afore, and that he couldna hae learnt any ither way than by turnin' wi' shame frae the path o' the transgressor. I hae brought him wi' me this day, to tell ye somethin'—he hasna said to me what—that the Lord in his mercy has telled him. I'll say nae more. Mr. Blatherwick, will ye please tell us what the Lord has put in yer mind to say?"

The soutar sat down and James got up, white and trembling a little. For a moment or two he was unable to speak, but at last he overcame his emotion, and falling at once into the old Scots tongue, he began.

"My frien's, I hae little right to stand up afore ye and say anything. For as some oo ye ken, if no afore, then at least noo frae what my frien' the soutar hae jist be tellin' ye, I was once a minister o' the kirk, but upon a time I behaved mysel' so ill that, when I came to my senses, I saw it my duty to withdraw frae it. But noo I seem to hae gotten some more light upon spiritual matters that I didna hae afore, and to ken some things I didna ken afore. Sae turnin' my back upon my past sin, and believin' God has forgiven me, and is willin' I should set my hand to his plough once more, I hae thought to make a new beginnin' here in a quiet humble fashion, tellin' ye somethin' o' what I hae begun, in the mercy o' God, to un'erstand a wee for mysel'. Sae noo, if ye'll turn, them o' ye that has brought yer books wi' ye, to the seventh chapter o' John's gospel, and the seventeenth verse, ye'll read wi' me what the Lord says there to the fowk o' Jerusalem: *If any man be willin' to do his will, he'll ken whether what I tell him comes frae God, or whether I say it only oot o' my ain head.* Look at it for yersel's, for that's what it says in the Greek, which is plainer than the English to them that un'erstand the auld Greek tongue. If anybody *be willin'* to do the will o' God, he'll ken whether my teachin' comes frae God, or I say it o' mysel'."

From that he went on to tell them that, if they kept trusting in God, and doing what Jesus told them, any mistake they made would but help them the better to understand what God and his son would have them do. The Lord gave them no promise, he said, of knowing what this or that man ought to do, but only of knowing what the man himself ought to do. He illustrated this by the rebuke the Lord gave Peter when he inquired into the will of God concerning his friend rather than himself.

The little congregation seemed to hang upon his words, and as they were going away thanked him heartily for thus talking to them.

28 / The Restoration

All through the winter James accompanied the soutar to his Sunday school, sometimes on his father's old gig-horse, but oftener on foot. His father would occasionally go also, and then the men of Stonecross began to go with the cottar and his wife; so that the little company of them gradually increased to about thirty men and women and about half as many children.

In general, the soutar gave a short opening address, but he always had "the minister" speak, and thus James Blatherwick, while encountering many hidden experiences, went through his apprenticeship in extemporary preaching. Hardly knowing how, he grew capable at length of following out a train of thought in his own mind even while he spoke, made all the more real and living and powerful by the sight of the eager faces of his humble friends fixed upon him, sometimes ever seeming to anticipate the things he was saying. He felt at times that he was almost able to see their thoughts taking reality and form to accompany him where he led them as he spoke; while the stream of his thought, as it disappeared from his consciousness and memory, seemed to settle in the minds of those who heard him, like seed cast on open soil—some of it, at least, to grow up in resolves and bring forth fruit.

And all along the road as the friends returned to their homes, now in darkness and rain, sometimes in wind and snow, they had such things to think of and talk about that the way never seemed long. Thus dwindled by degrees Blatherwick's self-reflection and self-seeking, and growing conscious of the divine life both in him and around him, he grew at the same time altogether less conscious of himself.

On one such homecoming, as his wife was helping him off with his wet boots, he looked up in her face and said, "To think, Isy, that here I am, a dull, selfish creature, so long striving for knowledge and influence only for myself, now at last grown able to feel in my heart all the way home that I took every step, one after the other, only by

the strength of God in me, caring for me as my own making Father!—
Do you know what I'm trying to say, Isy, my dear?"

"I can't be altogether certain I understand," she answered, "but
I'll keep thinking about it, and maybe I'll come to it."

"I can ask no more," said James, "for until the Lord lets you see
a thing, how can you or I or anybody see the thing that he must see
first. And what is there for us to desire but to see things as God sees
them and would have us see them? I used to think the soutar such a
simpleton when he was saying the very things that I'm trying to say
now. I saw no more what he was after than that poor collie there at
my feet—maybe not half so much, for who can tell what he might
not be thinking with that far away look of his!"

"Do you think, James, that we'll ever be able to see inside the
doggies, and know what they're thinking?"

"I wouldn't wonder what we might not come to. For you know
Paul says, 'All things are yours, and you are Christ's, and Christ is
God's!' Who can tell but that the very hearts of the doggies may one
day lie bare and open to *our* hearts as to the heart of him with whom
they and we have to do. Eh, but the thoughts of a doggie must be a
wonderful sight. And then to think of the thoughts of Christ about
that doggie! We'll know them, I don't doubt, someday. I'm surer
about that than about knowing the thoughts of the doggie himself!"

Another Sunday night, having come home through a terrible
storm of thunder and lightning, he said to Isy, "I have been feeling,
all the way home, as if before long I might have to give a wider
testimony. The apostles and the first Christians, you see, had to bear
testimony to the fact that the man that was hanged and died upon the
cross, the same was up again and out of the grave and going about
the world. Now I can't bear testimony to that, for I wasn't at that
time aware of anything. But I might be called upon to bear testimony
to the fact that, where once he lay dead and buried, there he's come
alive at last—that is, in the sepulchre of my heart! For I have seen
him now, and know him now—the hope of glory in my heart and
life. Whatever he said once, that I now believe forever!"

The talks James Blatherwick and the soutar had together were
wonderful. Occasionally Mr. Robertson joined them, for he still came
weekly to conduct services in the parish church. Whether it was the

two or the three of them gathered together, it was chiefly the cobbler that spoke, while James in particular sat and listened in silence. On one occasion, however, James had spoken out freely, and indeed eloquently, and Mr. Robertson, whom the cobbler accompanied to his inn that night spoke to him about James before they parted.

"Do you see any good reason, Mr. MacLear, why this man should not resume his pastoral office?"

"One thing at least I am sure of," answered the soutar, "—that he is far fitter for it than ever he was in his life before."

Mr. Robertson repeated this to James the next day, adding, "And I am certain everyone who knows you will vote for the restoration of your license."

"I must speak both to Isy and to the Lord about it," answered James with simplicity.

"That is quite right, of course," rejoined Mr. Robertson. "I tell my wife everything that I am at liberty to tell."

"Will not some public recognition of my reinstatement be necessary?" suggested James.

"I will have a talk with the leaders of the synod, and let you know what they say," answered Mr. Robertson.

"Of course I am ready," returned Blatherwick, "to make any public confession judged necessary or desirable; but that would involve my wife. And although I know perfectly well that she will be ready for anything required of her, it remains not the less my part to do my best to shield her. I do know, however, that restoration in the biblical sense goes in two directions. And it is not until I have made what restoration lies within my grasp to account for my sins that I can in any sense be publicly restored."

"You are quite right. The two go hand in hand, just as forgiveness must be born in God's heart and then bear fruit between fellow men and women. Of one thing I think you may be sure—that with our present moderator, your case will be handled with more than delicacy—with tenderness!"

"I do not doubt it! I appreciate your generosity. But make sure he knows that I am willing, not only to be restored, but also to make restoration to any others I may have hurt. I have tried to do so already, but he may request something public. But I must have a talk with my wife about it. She is sure to know what will be best."

"My advice is to leave it in the hands of the moderator. We have no right to choose, appoint, or apportion our own penalties. I will share your heart with him, and I know we can trust him to speak on behalf of the Lord."

James went home and laid the whole matter before his wife.

Instead of looking frightened, or even anxious, Isy laid little Peter softly in his crib, threw her arms round James's neck, and cried, "Thank God, my husband, that you have come to this! Don't leave me out of whatever confessions must be made, I beg of you. I am more than ready to accept my shame. I have always said I was to blame. It was I who should have known better!"

"You trusted me, and I proved quite unworthy of your confidence! But did ever a man have a wife to be so proud of as you!"

Mr. Robertson brought the matter carefully before the synod. But neither James nor Isy ever heard anything more of it—except the announcement of the cordial renewal of James's license. This was soon followed by the offer of a church in the poorest and most populous parish north of the Tweed.

"See the loving power at the heart of things, Isy!" said James to his wife. "Out of evil God has brought good, the best good, and nothing but the good!—a good ripened through my sin and selfishness and ambition, bringing upon you as well as me disgrace and suffering. The evil in me had to come out and show itself before it could be cleared away! Some people nothing but an earthquake will rouse from their dead sleep. I was one of such! God in his mercy brought on the earthquake to wake me and save me from death.

"Ignorant people go about always asking why God permits evil. *We* know why! So that we might come to know—really know!—what good is like, and therefore what God himself is like. It may be that he could with a word eliminate evil altogether and cause it to cease. But what would that teach us about good? The word might make us good like oxen or harmless sheep, but would that be a worthy image of him who was made in the image of God? For a man to cease to be *capable* of evil, he must cease to be man! What would the goodness be that could not help being good—that had no choice in the matter, but must be such because it was so made? God chooses to be good, otherwise he would not be God: Man must choose to be good, otherwise he cannot be the son of God."

"God *is* good, isn't he, James!"

"And so good to us! Just think where we each might be if he *hadn't* shown us ourselves, even in our sin. We might never have known his goodness had it not been for the evil in us."

"Oh, but that was such a hard time! To think that he was with us every step."

"That is how grand the love of the Father of men is, Isy—that he gives them a share, and that share as necessary as his own, in the making of themselves. Thus, and only thus, by willing—by choosing—the good, can they become partakers of the divine nature. All the discipline, all the pain of the world exists for the sake of this—that we may come to choose the good. God is teaching us to know good and evil in some real degree *as they are* and not as they *seem* to the incomplete. So shall we learn to choose the good and refuse the evil. He would make his children see the two things, good and evil, in some measure as they are, and then say whether they will be good children or not. If they fail, and choose the evil, he will take yet harder measures with them, salting them with continually deeper pains and cleansing of the refiner's fire.

"If at last it should prove possible for a created being to see good and evil as they are, and choose the evil, then, and only then, there would, I presume, be nothing left for God but to set his foot upon him and crush him as we might a noxious insect.

"But God is deeper in us than our own life. Yea, God's life is the very center and creative cause of that life which we call *ours*. Therefore is the Life in us stronger than the Death, inasmuch as the creating Good is stronger than the created Evil."